SOAKED HAY & STABLE MIRRORS

F W RIDER

DEDICATION

For my two beautiful daughters, Neve & Joss, who put up
with my head being in my laptop way more often than it
should be! You must never read this book... well, maybe
when you're both thirty!

SOAKED HAY & STABLE MIRRORS

Written by
F. W. Rider

If you'd like to find out more about forthcoming releases or the life of my equine army in general, check out my links below! You can also sign up to my free mailing list via my website!

Can you recognise a certain little mare in this story, who may pop up from time to time on my socials? If you do, let me know! She has a series coming of her very own!

Get to know me more here...
Instagram - https://www.
instagram.com/thefairweatherrider/
Facebook - https://www.facebook.com/thefairweatherrider
Website - http://thefairweatherrider.com

Due to the rather excessive use of profanity, graphic sexual references and adult subject matter, this book should only be read by those who aren't easily offended and should without a doubt be kept out of reach of anyone under the age of 18.

SOAKED HAY & STABLE MIRRORS

Book 2 of 2 in the Smoke & Mirrors Series

Written By
F.W. Rider

Contact info@thefairweatherrider.com for more
information on future releases.

ONE

MY EYELIDS FEEL HEAVY. My body feels even heavier. I'm lying against a hard, cold surface, but there's one thing that's keeping me from panicking and it's the familiar smell that's currently filling my nostrils. Horse. I can smell horse. I can hear horses too. I feel a little woozy, and part of me hopes that I've fallen from Lincoln and one of the girls has dragged me into his stable to sleep it off or something – not that they would, but it seems like a far more appealing idea than what I believe is actually going on.

I hear her before I see her. I feel her too. The walls dividing the stables must be pretty low because I know I'm on the floor and yet she can still reach me with ease. She sniffs me and blows warm air all over my face. I feel her whiskers gently bristle over my skin. I have no idea how I know she's a she, but I just do.

My eyelids start to respond to the signals from my very tired brain and begin to flicker open. I see a minuscule amount of light, but it's only slight. It's night time. I search my surroundings and see that I am indeed in a stable. My neck feels stiff, as if I've slept funny, but my body feels exhausted, as if it hasn't slept at all. There's bedding all around me and I'm propped up against the back wall. The stable door is directly in front of me, and the top half of it is open. I'm bloody freezing despite the huge coat that's currently drowning me. *Whose coat is this? Who put it on me?* Oh God, my head. It's throbbing.

My hand bumps into her nose as I draw it up to cup my aching forehead and she shoots back.

'Sorry, my love.'

She looks scared, but she can't be for long because she's back down, sniffing me and inspecting my fragile head once again. She looks thin. Too thin. Her neck is stick-like, and her coat is rough and coarse.

Even in the dark I can see she's a beautiful, albeit dull, chestnut with a thick white blaze that runs down her face and covers the whole of her muzzle. She's stunning, even in her emaciated state.

'Hi...' I manage to whisper as her muzzle rests on my shoulder, as if to comfort me in these strange surroundings. I should be petrified, but I'm not. I'm as calm as I think I've ever been in my life. Maybe this is what survival mode is. It's kicked in and my inner Buffy is going to emerge and kick some serious fucking arse.

In an effort to remain calm and try to keep myself as logical as possible, I'm listing everything that's happened. I don't know how I got here. I'm in a stable at night, and there's a fresh bed of straw around me. It's not like this has never happened before when Lincoln's had colic, only this time there's no Lincoln and there's certainly no reason for me to be here. My body and my head especially feel like they've been hit by a bus, and I'm struggling to understand just where the bloody hell I am or, more importantly, get up and walk out.

I was with Liv. *Where's Liv?* Yes, I'm certain I was out with Liv. I must have been. I've got my non-yard jeans on, jeans that aren't ever allowed to set foot near Lincoln, and I'm wearing my AllSaints boots. *I was at Hogan's.* That's all I can remember. I do wonder if that's all I *want* to remember and my body is just doing its job at keeping me calm and feeding me only the information it thinks I need to know rather than everything I can genuinely remember.

I look up once more and see a haynet next to the door. It's old.

I start to shuffle, trying to make it onto my feet, and she's there like a shot, watching over me as I stumble. I reach up slowly and grip the top line of the wall and pull myself up.

She's nudging me, like a horse who's been down for too long. She's telling me to get up too. She nickers quietly at me, encouraging me to my feet like a foal trying to stand for the first time, and I can't deny the noise comforts me. Knowing she's there makes me feel so much better, despite this godawful situation I seem to have found myself in.

I make it up to my feet, standing a little crooked, leaning on the wall. It's made of old wood. Probably old pallets. Despite its shabby appearance, it's more than sturdy enough to hold me up.

Her head lifts in front of me and her ears prick forward. She's on full alert. Her frail and withered body hasn't had a chance to catch up with her mind because she's without a doubt all there and far more aware than I am right now.

I start walking, or stumbling rather, to the front of the stable, and she's anything but happy about it. She has her head in front of me the whole way, darting back and forth between alert and in search of whatever she can hear outside and nudging me back. Curiosity overruns my desire to listen to her though and I continue moving forward. I reach the door and am met with a smell that's so putrid I feel even more nauseous than I already do.

The haylage in the haynet by the door must have been here for weeks and weeks. It's rotten, covered in mould and nothing short of vomit inducing. How is the bed fresh but the haynet rotten? Unless the bed was laid for me specifically?

I look over into her stable and it's filth. The straw has been pissed on for days. If not weeks. She's covered in excrement, and her net and water bowl are empty. By the smell of her muzzle, she's so hungry that she's started eating the piss-soaked straw bedding. I want to cry. Not for me but for her. She's a hat rack, as thin as anything I've ever seen, and yet she's still so loving toward me. We don't deserve animals. They're too good for us.

I usher myself forward some more and try to make my way to look outside, but I hear a noise first. My body moves before I tell it to, I'm sure. Now that's survival mode. The mare starts pacing and nickering a little louder. As if calling me closer, telling me to take shelter with her.

I look around the stable and all I see are four bare walls. There's nowhere to hide, and I'm in no fit state to run. The only thing I can think to do is to go back to where I was and pretend to be asleep again. They say to do that if you're about to be attacked by a bear and can't escape right? I don't feel in too dissimilar a situation right now. I just don't know what sort of bear I'm about to deal with.

I stagger back, haphazardly, to my previous cold corner and flop back into position, then prop myself up against the back wall and close my eyes. She's back smelling me and comforting me more than she realises as I hear scuffles outside and the metal latch on the stable door slide open. It opens with a clunk, and I feel a breeze rush in as the door opens.

'She's in here.'

'What the hell did you do? Why the fuck have you brought her here?'

There are two voices. One is vaguely familiar. A woman's voice. The other is male. I don't know it.

'You told me to sort it, so I did.'

'No! I told you to sort it out, get her to back off. I didn't fucking say kidnap her. Did I? Did I give you those specific instructions? Jesus Christ, Angel, what have you done?'

Well that clears that one up. I'm shaking through fear at what's happening right now though I have a feeling the oversized coat is keeping that hidden. Even if they can see it, it'll look as if I'm shivering from the cold, or at least I hope it will. The last thing I need is for them to know I can actually hear every word they say. I don't need them 'dealing' with me in any different manner than they already have. This is hell and I want out, but right now I need to keep quiet, keep my mouth shut and wait this out.

'I thought you could have a word with her, scare her a bit, and she'll probably drop the journo thing and piss off. What's so wrong about that?'

'Because this takes things into a whole new league, you moron. If you ever wonder why we pimp you out, you stupid little slag, it's because that's all you're good for. Well done, Angel – another cock-up yet again.'

'Wait, I wanted to show you that I could hold my own. Eddie doesn't even know...'

The voices drop off, and the space around me is once again filled with silence. The air is heavy and my breathing laboured after what I've just heard. Angel has kidnapped me and brought me here, to her brothers. I'm assuming the male voice belonged to one of them. I guess when Eddie said this was dangerous, he wasn't exaggerating. I feel sick, and the panic in me starts to rise. *What the hell do I do now?*

I need to get out of here – and fast.

The thought of quickly lassoing the nearest horse, jumping aboard and galloping out of here while Angel and her cronies are in hot pursuit flashes through my mind like some godawful western film from the fifties, but I quickly remind myself that not only do I not have a clue about the horse next to me, but I'm pretty sure she'd struggle to carry herself, let alone me as well. Plus, the fact that I can barely hold myself up is somewhat of an issue. I've only been around her what feels like minutes but I'm also acutely aware of the fact that I can't leave her.

I look up at her face again and see eyes that are not only full of pain and anguish but full of love. For me. A total stranger.

'Don't worry, babe. We'll get out of here together. I won't leave you.'

She nods at me, as if she's understood every single word I've said. But then again, why wouldn't she? Lincoln does, on a daily basis no less; I'm sure of it.

Just like that, our bond is sealed and I start trying to figure out what the bloody hell I can do.

TWO

I START SEARCHING the pockets of the coat I'm wearing. They're empty. I have no phone. No wallet. I have nothing. I have no way of getting out of here with this mare in tow, and I'm pretty sure neither of us are capable of walking very far, even if we could just up and leave with a vague clue of where we're going.

I get up on my feet, this time a little more easily than before, and make my way to the stable door. I peer out into the darkness and see a light coming from what looks like an office about thirty yards to the left of me. I look ahead and in the distance, maybe half a mile away, I see a huge windmill or something. Are there street lights lighting it up or is it lit up itself? I'm not sure but it's huge. It's either a windmill or some kind of lighthouse... in the middle of dry land. I have no idea what I'm looking at, but either way, it's of no use.

The stable door is swinging open from when they walked away earlier. They were careless. If they were careless with that, then they've been careless elsewhere – or at least I hope they have.

I step out of the stable door, keeping myself as close to

the wall as possible. There's a dull light above me and I'm aware that I don't want to create shadows down toward where Angel and that man are. I'd rather not find out her intentions at this precise moment in time. I'd rather wait until I have the strength to at least swing a fist at her smug, shitty little face.

As I creep past the mare's door, she pops her head over, watching me and nickering as I walk across her threshold and continue to the building beyond her. She either wants my attention or she's telling me this is a bad idea. Whatever her message, I ignore her completely and continue on my way. I'm looking for something. Anything. Something to help me get out of here.

I walk three stable doors away from the now box-walking mare and stumble upon what looks like a dusty, mice-infested office. The door's unlocked and there's a phone and laptop on the table. Our gateway out of here. With fingers crossed, I slowly walk toward the phone and lift it, praying to the god of all things good that I hear a dialling tone, but it's dead.

'Fuck's sake, you piece of shit.' I throw the phone down and open the laptop. The screen's black and there appears to be no life, but I press the button to turn it on anyway, and as if by magic, that beautiful piece of fruit fills my screen like a beacon of hope. It loads up pretty quickly and shows me there's only five per cent battery left. I hop onto Facebook and immediately message my mum and Liv. I tell them I'm lost. I'm at stables in what could very well be the middle of nowhere. My legs feel heavy and I can't run, but there's also a mare here that needs to come with me.

Liv messages back within seconds.

Liv: Fuck, Jen! The police are looking for you. You just disappeared. Can you see anything?

Jen: It's dark but I'm sure I can see a water tower or a windmill, something like that.

Liv: Can you do 'find my location' or something on whatever device you're on?

Jen: Two secs...

I open another window, noting the battery has already dropped down to a pathetic two per cent and type in 'find my location', mouthing it as I do. A few different options click up but I choose the top one.

I hear the mare nickering from afar as I click the website, asking it to tell me exactly where I am. I get coordinates which make no sense whatsoever, swiftly followed by a street address.

The Birds, Lavender Way, Langley. I'm not far at least.

Jen: The Birds, Lavender Way, Langley. Get help! And a trailer. Get a car and trailer or a horsebox! The mare can't stay here.

Liv: On it, hang tight. I'm calling Eddie.

Jen: Do not call Eddie. Call my mum and tell her I'm OK and...

And before I can finish the message and send, the laptop dies on me. Shit. If she calls Eddie, he might even alert these guys. Is he in on this? It's the first time since I came to, that I've even considered the possibility. Has he done this with Angel? Does he know about it?

I make my way back to the mare's stable and let myself in. There's a headcollar and lead rope hanging outside which I grab hold of as I lean over the door and lock it shut. I turn to put it over her head and she's shot to the back of the stable. She's skittish suddenly. I wonder whether she's been subject to some heavy hands inside the stable and consider whether I'd be better off putting the headcollar on her over the wall from where I stood before.

'It's OK, my love. It's OK,' I reassure her in my most soothing voice and turn to walk out of the stable.

I don't know this mare. She looks just a few days away from death's door, especially with a complete lack of water or feed, but she could turn on me out of fear at any moment, and in the state I'm in, my reactions won't be quick enough to avoid a swift kick so I'm going to err on the side of caution.

I make my way out of the stable and back to where I originally was. She immediately calms and makes her way to the partition, invading my space as soon as she's able to. I pop the headcollar on to her thin and bony-looking face with ease. It hangs off of her cheekbones and below her jaw, showing that it once likely fit her perfectly.

I hear a telephone ring in the distance and hear angry voices. There's shouting. Both male and female voices. The mare lifts her head and starts looking out to where the light was coming from earlier, and right on cue, I hear doors slamming and footsteps heading my way.

Without thinking, I throw myself over the partition and into her stable. She spooks immediately and shoots to the other side of the stable, watching my every movement. She's petrified, but right now I'd rather take a swift boot from her than find myself at the mercy of whoever decided to abduct me with Angel, because it without a doubt took more than her to get me here.

I hide down in her stable and make myself as small as I possibly can. She looks as nervous as I feel, but something in her shifts as she sees my fear isn't directed at her but rather whoever's coming toward her stable. She backs toward me and lifts her head in the air. Her ears thrash back and forward as she keeps track of what's happening in front of her and what's happening behind her, or in other words, my quivering wreck of a self hiding in a pile of straw in the dark and dingy corner. Despite her unease and my fear, I'm essentially covered by her, though I'm curious to know whether she's done this on purpose? Does she know on some level what's happening? Is she looking at me akin to a foal that she needs to protect? Either way, I'm grateful for whatever it is that she's doing.

The footsteps get louder, and as they do, the mare becomes more erratic – pacing back and forth, weaving from side to side. I hear them walk into the stable I was originally out cold in and the footsteps stop.

'Where the fuck is she? Where is she, Angel?'

'I don't know! She should have still been out cold.'

I hear straw flying around the stable and the mare backs into me as I see something fly through the air. It looks like an arm comes toward her, and I hear a low growl from the male. She's now almost sitting on me. Her thighs look so incredibly thin, but the warmth coming off of her right now, both literally and figuratively, is overwhelming.

She's protecting me – it's undeniable. I don't care what people say about these creatures not having feelings or not knowing what's going on. She knows full well, and despite her pitiful state, she's doing everything in her power to keep me safe. I cannot leave her here.

I'm shaking with fear and so is she. We stand as still as possible. All I can hear is both of our breathing, although hers sounds a hell of a lot more laboured than mine right now. I hear car doors shutting in the distance and a lot of yelling, but I can't make out what's being said. I do know, however, there seems to be more than just Angel and this guy. Maybe another guy? Could it be another one of her brothers? Please don't let it be Eddie that's out there now, searching for me. I can only hazard a guess, but that seems like a sure bet at the moment. I need to get out of here, and I need to get out of here with an emaciated horse who doesn't look like she could walk very far if she tried.

I wait for her to move, fearful that any sudden movement from me could see that hock that's currently almost resting on my face doing some serious damage. It's almost like she reads my mind though, or perhaps reads my now steadier breathing because she moves forward and turns toward me, sniffing me once again. I rise to my feet, very conscious of her last unease at me being in the stable with her, but she's not as anxious this time. She's by no means relaxed, but it would seem we've bonded over our mutual fear of the people she hates the most. The people who've starved her.

I move toward the stable door, keeping low and trying my best to keep my breathing as steady as it was before. I'm conscious that I need to remain calm and steady for her as much as I do myself.

I peer out of the stable door and look toward the lit room they were congregating in before. Nothing. The lights are still on, but I can't see anyone through the windows or at least where they previously were. It's time to get out of here.

I grab the lead rope and turn to the mare. The sun has begun to rise, which has given me an ounce of extra light, allowing me to see the outline of a few scars on her face as well as a nameplate. Hattie.

'So your name's Hattie, is it?'

She nuzzles into my arm and nickers some more. She's relaxed. She must know it's time to go.

I move slowly and steadily, so as not to take her out of this relaxed and rather trusting state, and clip the lead rope onto her headcollar. The door leans down somewhat on the bolt, so I push the toe of my boot under the door and lift it millimetres, enough to allow me to open the bolt silently. I don't need to alert anyone to our movement. I want to walk out of here as quickly as possible. I look at her hooves and sigh in relief as I note she's barefoot. Thank God. She's going to be much quieter walking out of here with me.

One more sweep across the yard and I note it's still dead and free of anyone that could possibly see our exit. I open the door and gently cluck her to follow me, though it would seem she needs no encouragement as she's by my side the second I step my right foot forward. I'm exhausted, but adrenaline is pumping through my body thanks to the fear of someone seeing us and me not being able to run.

We take a right turn out of her stable, away from the office, and head to a huge five-bar gate. There's a lock on it, but there's also a smaller gate to the right. It's unlocked, and in her skin-and-bone state, she passes through it with ease. We're out.

The sun may be starting to rise but it's still fairly dark out here which makes the headlights in front of me difficult to miss. *Fuck!* They must have seen us. I look behind me in a panic and search for anywhere to go, but there isn't. It's one long straight road and we're out in the open for all to see.

Before I run and attempt to jump the ditch to my left, I see the truck coming toward me... with a trailer attached. It's Eddie.

Panic rises up inside of me. While deep down I'm sure he wouldn't have anything to do with this, whether I like it or not, he is linked to them, so it's possible I could be wrong and he knows exactly what's going on right now.

There's a car behind him too. With lights. A police car. But there are no sirens whatsoever.

Eddie's truck comes to a screeching halt and the trailer

behind him looks like it's about to jackknife at the rapid speed he made it stop. The mare, Hattie, looks absolutely petrified and backs up, snorting at what's happening right in front of her.

Eddie looks sick with fear. He opens the door to his truck and throws his body out quicker than I've ever seen him move before, but that's it. My vision starts to blur and the noise around me becomes muffled. I sit myself on the tarmac, lowering myself by holding on to the mare, before I fall down, and lay my head on the ground. I'm going to be OK. We're going to be OK.

THREE

'YOU'RE OK NOW, JEN.'

'You're fine now.'

I hear everything around me. The lights may be off, but there's still very much someone at home. I'm home. I hear the bleeps of machines, and I hear familiar voices. That's all they feel like though. Familiar.

'How are you feeling, love?'

'Lincoln's fine. The girls are looking after him.'

I can hear these voices though I have no desire to respond just yet, but my body is telling me I need to.

My eyes blink and the light invades my once calm and rather serene being. I'm waking up. *Why was I asleep?*

As I begin to blink and the world appears around me, I hear those familiar voices getting louder and more frantic. It's Mum. And Liv.

'Jen, look at me, sweetheart; look at me. Honey, are you OK?'

'Oh my God, are you OK? Jen?' I hear Liv sob.

My mum's voice has a tinge of anger in there, though I

know it's not aimed at me. My vision is blurry and I wonder where the hell I am.

As the sights in front of me begin to gain a little more clarity, I soon realise I'm in hospital.

I want to talk but I feel absolutely shattered, and in all honesty, I'd rather just look at Mum and Liv. Hold their hands and let the relief that's apparent on their faces wash over me. I'm safe... but when wasn't I?

'My God, honey, you had us worried. I was petrified. I'm so glad—' She cuts off and tries to stop herself from crying, but she doesn't quite manage it, and the rest comes out in an inaudible sob.

'Mum, I'm OK. I'm fine. Please don't get upset.'

'I can't help but think what could have happened to you in—' She breaks off into another high-pitched, inaudible tone.

It's breaking my heart to see her like this, but right now, I'm more curious than ever about what's going on. I look to Liv and instinctively she knows I'm searching for answers.

'Right, OK, so Lincoln is being looked after by the girls. You know, the ones you chat to and ride with. One of them has that bastard little demon pony thing that tries to take chunks out of you. You know?'

'Yeah,' I just about squeeze out.

'Umm, so when I got that Facebook message, umm, I rang Eddie. Told him you'd messaged me and that you had a mare. He thought it might have been one of the, you know... them? But I said you'd said you needed a trailer or some-thing so if you were rescuing a fucking horse, it was defi-nitely you, but he wouldn't let me come, and I'd been drinking at Hogan's so I couldn't drive. The police picked up your mum, and by the time Eddie had whacked a trailer on the back of his truck, they'd caught up with him. That's when they found you in the road with that hat rack of a horse.'

'The mare... umm, Hattie. Where is she? Is she OK?'

'Eddie just loaded her up. Told the police he was taking her to a local sanctuary and they just went with it. In all honesty, I think they just looked the other way and dealt with you because, let's face it, you're more than enough trouble.'

Her usual one-sided grin sweeps across her face as she says it, and I can't help but laugh. I feel relief that I'm away from there and am incredibly grateful that aside from a few bruises and aches from being left on a cold stable floor, I'm absolutely fine. It could have been much worse.

Just as I'm about to start telling them how much I love them, there's a knock at the door. I can't help but jump. I guess I'm still on edge from being abducted by that bitch Angel. The door opens and two men in suits and long dress coats walk in.

The tall one speaks first. 'Hi, we're here to speak with Jen Seaton. We saw through the window that you were awake. Thought it would be a good time to ask some questions.'

He looks like a cocky fuck. I instantly hate the look of him. He seems way too sure of himself and not at all the type of person who's aware of what's just happened. If he is, he doesn't give a shit.

The second guy looks at both Mum and Liv, almost urging them to leave the room. He nods to the door with a smile on his face.

My mum, bless her heart, stands taller, holding my hand, and shoots him down. 'Do you have any idea what she's been through and now you're here, wanting to ask her questions and have us leave her alone – AGAIN?'

'Mum, it's OK. It's fine. Go grab me a cuppa, and maybe a bite to eat or something. I'm bloody starving. I'll talk to these guys and then you can take me home. Please?'

The tall one does his best to look a little less smug and pacify my mum but tells her, 'We just need to ask some routine questions. We won't take long at all. Then I'm sure the doctors will be ready to discharge your daughter and you can take her home.'

I give her one last look before she nods. Liv looks to me to give her the nod too. I do, and they both pick their bags up and make their way out of the room. I look to the side of me to grab a cup of water and notice that Liv has left her phone there.

Turning to the door, I see she's already gone so make a mental note to remind her when she comes back.

'Seems like you've had quite the ordeal, Miss Seaton?'

I'm guessing he's gone through life with a chip on his shoulder about something because his desire to lord it over me while I'm in a hospital bed, following an abduction, is disturbing. I'm not sure if he's pissed off at being a good six inches shorter than his partner or if he's just sick to death of looking the lesser evil of the two, but his slicked-back hair makes him look more corrupt investment banker rather than bent copper.

'Are you always so smarmy to casualties or is it just me that you've taken a dislike to?'

The taller one has a moody look on his face and a shabby five o'clock shadow. He looks tired but he's trying his best to appear imposing. He's standing at the end of my bed and grabs my folder of notes and begins to flick through them. It's instantly obvious these guys are the 'friends in high places' Tristan has previously spoken about.

Strangely enough, I'm not fearful at all. In fact, if

anything, I just feel pissed off right now, and my blood is beginning to boil.

'Well now, Jennifer, that's no way to talk to the authorities.'

'And that's who you are, is it? See now, I just thought you were a couple of wankers on the Drafter brothers' payroll?'

They look at me for a moment in silence – I guess deciding how they're going to play this.

'Ooh, that's hit a nerve I'm guessing. Wondering how to play it now? I gather you thought you could probably walk in here, carry on with this condescending shit and frighten me into keeping my *pretty little nose out?*

'I must apologise for misleading you. While I do appear to be a little lady, all five-foot-six of me happens to be a rather nosey fucker, and while I may have been through quite the ordeal, I'm far more curious now than ever of what's going on. I have a job to do, and I'm going to do it. I *will* find out what's going on, and when I do, I'll be sure to send the police your way.'

'You seem to be mistaken, Jen; we are the police.'

'Ah in that case, *you* seem to be mistaken. I meant the decent ones. You might be able to throw your weight around and get what you want now, but believe me, when I'm done with this, you guys are going to be fucked.'

Sensing they were getting nowhere fast, the taller muppet of the two tries a different approach. 'What makes you think we're not decent police officers?'

'It might have something to do with the fact that you came in here uninvited and requested to speak with me alone. It may also have something to do with the fact that you've shown no ID, haven't informed me of your names and, worse still, both look like utter pieces of shit.'

'Look, I can see we're getting nowhere fast, so let's get to the point, shall we? Sadly, the investigation surrounding what happened to you will end before it's even begun. I'll make sure of it. No evidence you see; plus you had alcohol in your system. As far as I'm aware, a nosey slag like you probably lured some bloke to that stable for a quick shag and is now too embarrassed to admit what she did.'

I bite my tongue, refusing to rise to this bullshit as the short arse now decides to interject.

'Now, I don't want us to get off on the wrong foot here, but let's make some things very clear. We don't like people snooping around our business. In fact, we hate it. We hate it so much that we tend to make those nosey bastards' lives hell, and we'll do exactly the same for you. If you continue to nose around our business and cause our friends problems, we'll be forced to make your life very difficult. If you really piss us off, we'll do the same for your friends and family. I mean, Jen, let's get real now. Your mum, bless her heart, lives all alone. Your friend Liv looks a spunky one, but from what we've heard from Damion, she's anything but. And then there's Eddie. Your little boyfriend isn't who you think he is. He's on our side with this shit.

'Let's not forget that stupid brain-dead horse of yours either. He's at that stable yard, all alone at night, with only a few other horses for company. Would be too easy to slip something in there and wave goodbye to that dumb animal wouldn't it? That's not even mentioning the theft of a chestnut mare yesterday. Those sort of charges would ruin your career, wouldn't they? I mean the defence costs would be astronomical – you'd never recover. Living like that, always looking over your shoulder, wondering whether someone's loosened the nuts of your car wheels... it's not worth it, is it?'

'You can pull this crap as much as you want – it's not working. Plus, let's not forget, I'm pretty sure you have more than enough errands for your 'friends' to keep you too busy to keep on top of my whereabouts.'

'Oh, don't you worry, Miss Seaton.' He leans over me in bed and does his best to appear as threatening as possible. 'We'll know exactly where you are, every minute of the day.' With that, he throws my phone on the bed and nods to his partner. The taller guy blows me a kiss and they make their way to the door of my room.

'You still haven't told me your names...'

'I tell ya what, let's say we'll introduce ourselves fully if we need to pay you another visit?'

Despite my attempts at trying to stand my ground, I'm physically shaking. I'm absolutely petrified, and I'm guessing by the smug look on their faces, my big chat did nothing to hide that fact.

It would appear I was glaringly obvious in the fact that I was all mouth and most certainly no trousers.

FOUR

THEY MUST HAVE BEEN WAITING OUTSIDE because it's not even a minute after the two wankers have left that my mum and Liv appear.

'So what was all that about?' Liv dives straight in.

'They're the "friends in high places" I've been informed the Drafter brothers have.' I try for a half-smile to put my mum at rest. I can see she's uneasy about it all, and it's no surprise either. Her only child has just been threatened by the very people who are supposed to protect us. I can't say she's the only one feeling the unease right now, but I don't want her to know that.

She comes to my side and puts her arm around me. I was stupid to think I could fool her. She's my mum. We know each other inside and out. She knows exactly how I'm feeling, and we're both now doing our best to make the other one feel better. It's ridiculous and heart-warming at the same time.

'I love you, Mum.'

'I love you too, my babe.'

Rubbing my shoulder, I lean into her neck before

turning around to see what Liv is up to. She's picking up her phone.

'I was going to shout you to grab your phone but you'd already left the room.'

'I left it in here on purpose, my little investigative journo!'

'What do you mean?'

She starts swiping her finger up and down the screen before smiling to herself and poking her tongue out at me. 'You're not the only one who can *investigate*, you know!'

I'm genuinely flummoxed. 'What are you on about?'

'I recorded the twats, didn't I?' Her smile is getting bigger by the minute as she swipes a few more times and holds it out for us to hear the entire conversation between myself and Bill and Ben the twat-like henchmen.

'Oh my God, Liv...' I'm stuck for something to say that isn't the most clichéd response but all I can think to say is, 'This is huge!'

'I'll send it to you so you have a copy. I'll send it to my own email too. Then do with it what you will.'

'They have logs of everyone who comes in here, along with cameras and stuff, so I'm guessing we'll be able to find out who they are pretty easily. The question is: will I be able to use it to find out more about what's actually going on?'

'You're not going to carry on doing this, are you?' My mum sounds worried, and I understand, but I can't just let this go.

'Mum, I need to do this. Look at what they did to me!'

'Yes, exactly, my babe. Look at what they did to you...' And as if she's been holding it in this entire time, she starts to sob.

'Oh, Mum.'

I throw my arms around her, but I can't reach her well so I pull the monitor off of me and move closer to her.

'I promise I'll be fine. I know what these guys are capable of now. I'm aware. I'll take the proper precautions and get more help. Please, Mum, you knew this was the stuff I was getting involved with. I can't walk away from it now.'

She looks at me with pleading eyes, but I can see she's having a battle with herself. She's trying her best to be a caring mother, one who wants to look after me and make sure I'm safe, but at the same time, she's desperately trying not to hold me back. I can only imagine what's going through her mind, but at the same time, I don't want to. I don't want the guilt of knowing the turmoil I'm causing. This job is important to me and I need to get it done. I will get it done.

My phone bleeps as it receives the voice recording from Liv. I go into my messages and notice I have some from Eddie that I don't recognise. They've been read but I'm guessing not by me – probably by the arseholes who paid me a visit earlier.

Eddie must have sent me fifty or more messages and rung me at least twice that. He seems desperate in his messages – to find out if I'm OK, where I am.

My finger hovers over the reply tab. Should I let him know I'm OK? Of course I should, but a thought enters my mind and unnerves me. If they had my phone, they may well have done something to it. They may also have his. They could quite easily be keeping tabs on me and I'd rather they didn't see the messages between him and I.

'Liv, can you do me a favour?'

'Anything, chick.'

'I need a new phone. Well I need a new SIM, with

minutes, data, etc. I've got an old phone at home that I can use. I don't want to use this one.'

'Yup, I can do that. Where are you heading now? Your mum's?'

'Yes. Why don't you come home with me, honey?' my mum says.

'Yeah, OK. But I need to go home first thing tomorrow.'

She nods and smiles, and I know I've instantly made her feel better. She's happy knowing she can take me home, take care of me for the night. Feed me up and make me feel better. Then tomorrow I can get back home and start where I left off, only this time, I have a lot more information.

You'd think right now I'd be scared, but I have a sudden determination. I'm in this, and no matter what they throw at me, I'm going to come back harder. I've got these guys. I'm on to them because I was already involved with Eddie. They must be worried to be doing what they're doing, but instead of frightening me off, they're making me even more determined than ever.

FIVE

AFTER I WAS DISCHARGED, Mum took me home, and we spent the evening with her hovering over me. She cooked me a roast dinner, which I vacuumed up quicker than even she thought I would. We then huddled on the sofa and watched two American teen romcoms with tea, biscuits and couple of glasses of wine. We laughed, we cried and we laughed some more. Then we both went to bed declaring to the other how much we loved each other, and, surprisingly enough, the pair of us slept more soundly than we'd expected. I woke up refreshed and feeling ready for war.

I told Mum I'd relax, though I suspect she knew I wasn't telling the whole truth, but she went along with it anyway. The car journey home was tough. She was quiet, worried about dropping me off alone, and I spent most of my time wondering what I'd do first.

I kiss Mum goodbye as she pulls up to the kerb, grab my things – which I've chucked in one of her overnight bags – and promise to call her in an hour to let her know I'm fine... and every other hour thereafter too, I might add.

I walk up the stairwell to the front door, put my key in and breathe a huge sigh of relief as I step across the threshold. Home. I'm home.

I make it my mission to try to actually get my body to relax. I soak in the bath with some of my favourite oils. I apply a hair mask and face mask. I scrub to within an inch of my life. I shave every square inch of my body, and apply lashings of my favourite lotion. I feel positively glowing and ready to relax in front of the TV, on my own with some comfort food and a film, but I can't. I'm restless.

The mare. I can't stop thinking about the mare, but at the same time I don't want to contact Eddie. I'm still not entirely sure how I feel. I know he came to me when I needed him, but was he part of it all? Was it all just part of the plan to keep me telling him what I'm doing so they have all the information they need to keep me away? Did he lead them to me?

I'm staring at the ceiling, with every thought possible flying through my head. I make a mental note to reply to the emails from Tristan. He's emailed multiple times, telling me he came to the hospital but he wasn't allowed in. He's also told me to not bother calling him back and to take a few days, though he wants to visit me at some point to make sure I'm OK. I just hope he doesn't want to take me off the story. I want to finish what I started. Or should that be barely started.

As my mind begins to trail off on a multitude of different thoughts, all unfortunately work related, I hear the buzzer go.

I figure it must be Mum. 'You couldn't leave me alone for one night, could you?' I say, chuckling to myself as I imagine her outside, worrying if I'm OK up here alone. I stick the kettle on as I head over to let her in – no doubt she'll want a cuppa.

But I'm rudely awaken from my relaxed state when I hear his voice. 'Can you let me in, Jen?'

'Why are you here?'

'Can you just let me in please? We need to talk. Plus I reckon you're going to want to know about that horse you had me steal.'

Bastard. He had to use her, didn't he?

I buzz him in and give myself a quick once-over in the mirror before unlocking the front door. He's just venturing up the top steps as I open it, and he looks me straight in the eye. He looks sad. Exhausted and sad.

I instantly feel relief just seeing him, but I'm mad still. Or at least I am until I see he's walking stiff. He's covered in bruises.

'I guess I don't need to ask what the hell happened to you?'

But instead of answering me, he simply walks straight toward me, cups my face with both of his grazed hands and kisses me. He kisses me hard.

As much as I want to resist him, to fight him off, I don't. For the simple fact I want him. I want his touch, I want his lips on me and I want to feel his hands all over.

He pulls away and searches my face for a reaction of some kind, but I don't give one.

Instead I simply ask, 'So where's my horse?' A diversion, no doubt, on my part.

He chuckles and I see the relief as his shoulders soften, and he throws his arms around me, engulfing me whole. His huge body and cocky demeanour only covers his soft and caring heart. I can't ignore the fact that he did come for me when I needed him. Flashes of his face enter my mind. I remember him looking almost sick with worry.

'What happened? How did you find me?'

'Liv called me after you gave her an address. Do you remember?'

'Yeah, I do now. I keep forgetting things and then it comes back to me. Where's the mare? Is she safe?'

'Yeah. She's actually at your yard. I've just come from there. Had a vet look at her yesterday. Apart from the emaciated state and her obvious nerves, she's actually in OK shape. She'll be fine with some care and attention. She's two stables down from Lincoln in that spare one everyone was using as a feed room. I put a stable mirror in there so she has someone to look at. She looks pretty relaxed when there are no people around. Your mates have been chucking over ad-lib hay. But we've been keeping it in small amounts at the minute, otherwise she just tries to stuff her face. Not really a surprise I guess, but I don't want to blast her stomach just yet, so we're building her up slowly but surely. She's being kept in for now and then the vet's going to check her again in a few days and make sure everything's OK to worm her.'

'Why haven't they wormed her yet?' I step back and make my way into the living room. I sit myself down on the sofa and then hear the kettle click. As I go to stand, he pushes me back down on the sofa, throws the blanket on me and makes his way into the kitchen.

'They're just taking things slow,' he shouts over his shoulder. 'Making sure she's in good enough condition before they pump a load of chemicals in and stuff. It's pretty standard. She's covered in lice too, which isn't helping with her weight, but I've bathed her in some stuff to get rid of the live ones. When the vet comes back, she's going to check if she's well enough to give her an injection to get rid of the rest. She'll be fighting fit before you know it.'

He's shouting from the kitchen, though he needn't bother. My flat isn't huge, so I can see and hear him quite clearly. I watch as he searches the cupboards, looking for mugs. I see a smile creep across his face as he finds my mugs – all character mugs that perfectly display my childish side.

'Thanks. For looking after her. And for coming for me too.' I hesitate for a second, then ask, 'Why did you leave it so long before you came to see me? You didn't come to the hospital?'

'In all honesty, I thought your mum would have killed me. But Liv kept me up to date with everything that went on, and as you've probably noticed, I had a few wounds of my own to deal with.' He looks at his hands and shrugs. 'To be expected I guess.

'After she contacted me on Facebook that night, I gave her my number and she's been letting me know that you're OK, where you are and stuff. She wanted to come here tonight,' he says, straining as he lowers himself to put the milk back on the bottom shelf of my fridge, 'but I told her I needed to see you and talk with you, so she gave us some space. She also gave me this to give to you...' He wanders in with two cups of tea in one hand and an envelope in another.

'What is it?' His curiosity gets the better of him as he hands it over to me.

'It's a new SIM. The guys that paid me the visit in hospital gave me back my phone and now, shock horror, I don't trust using it. Feel like they've bugged it or something.'

'That's why you never got back to me. I thought you hated me.'

He sits next to me and pulls my legs up over his, placing

his mug on the coffee table next to the sofa, and starts rubbing my feet.

'I was really fucking scared, Jen.' His voice breaks and I hear the heartache in him. I feel responsible for his current dose of bruises, by getting involved in this when he asked me not to, but I can't stay away now. I can't keep away from this, knowing what's going on. Knowing what they're capable of. It's killing me, not doing anything now.

'You need to tell me what's going on. Why you're covered in bruises and your hands – they're torn up.'

'They weren't happy about me coming to get you. 'My girlfriend getting involved in their business' is how they put it.'

I look past the term girlfriend and casually breeze on, even though my heart is doing somersaults. 'And everything else?'

'I just need some more time. You need to trust me, Jen. Please just trust me.'

'You're making it really difficult to do that,' I sigh with a heavy heart but ultimately decide to concede this one, just this once.

'I don't want to talk about what happened right now then. If you're not going to be truthful with me, I don't want to discuss it. I don't want to talk about how I felt being there. I don't even want to talk about what I intend to do tomorrow. I don't want to talk about those marks on you, and I certainly don't want to talk about you using the word girlfriend, for fuck's sake.

'I just want to sit here and watch shit on TV and eat shit food. If you're up for that, I'd like it if you stayed.'

The look of surprise on his face is quickly replaced by a huge smile, albeit a slightly tarnished one given the huge laceration running down the middle of his lip.

'Hang on a minute, did the uptight Jen Seaton just ask me for a cosy date night in on the sofa?'

'Yes she did, and the uptight Jen Seaton also likes biscuits with her tea, swiftly followed by a curry from the Raj, so chop-chop, Ed!'

'For so long I thought I knew you, but I had no idea how fucking resilient you are. You are one tough cookie, Jen.'

He rises from his seat, hovers over me and lands a kiss on my forehead. Delicate and almost friendly, but I hear him smell my hair and murmur, 'Coconut,' as he wanders into the kitchen to grab the biscuits.

'I'm a hungry one too so crack on, won't ya? I'm too weak to dial for a takeaway.'

And just like that, we do what we're oh so good at: forget what's happening outside the four walls of my flat and pretend it's just us. The connection is there, the feelings are very much there, and we're there – together.

SIX

I WAKE up feeling even more tired than I did when I went to bed. Eddie is lying next to me, though he's snuggled up on approximately a fifth of my bed, with me taking up the rest. He's holding my hand in his sleep. I feel content and uneasy all at the same time, and the anxiety only worsens when my buzzer goes again. Who the hell is it now?

Eddie jumps awake at the harsh sound and I tell him to lie back down, but he doesn't. 'Move. Let me see who it is first.'

'For fuck's sake, this is my apartment and I don't need bloody saving...' I look at him as he turns to me. 'Not today anyway.' I roll my eyes and push past him.

'Who is it?'

'Hello, gorgeous, it's your favourite boss. You going to let me in or what? I have chocolate croissants here, and they're still warm.'

'Hey, Tristan, come on up.' I buzz him up and look at Eddie, who I can see isn't exactly happy about this morning interruption.

'I guess that's the editor that's been getting you in trouble?'

'No, actually, that would be the editor who's given me a potentially huge break in my career. Be nice or fuck off – it's that simple.'

'Wow, you're back. That chilled version of you last night was great while it lasted.'

'As was the nice version of you, yet here we are with you acting a wanker before he's even stepped foot in my flat.'

I cock my head and see him trying to think of a retort. None come to him I'm guessing as he turns around and heads back to my bedroom. He's currently in just his pants, though nothing happened last night... as much as he may have wanted it to. I was far too full of bad food, and tiredness set in fairly early. I was hoping for a little morning action, as was Eddie I can see from the tent-pole-like action in his boxers, but Tristan has certainly put a stop to those plans. Might actually be a good idea while I gather my head and try my best to look at what's going on with this story, from as unbiased a viewpoint as possible.

While I don't like to admit it, Eddie is involved, and what's more, he's hiding as much as he can from me. I'm not happy about it, and I need to find out what's going on, not only for my own sanity but for this story too.

What I'd like to know is why I haven't been approached by any other law enforcement agents regarding what's happened. Has this been swept under the rug? We all know who's involved. Why can't they just arrest them?

A small knock at my front door brings me out of my own thoughts, and I'm suddenly aware that I'm now about to be alone in the same flat with Tristan and Eddie. This might not be the best idea, but it's about to happen, so I'm going to have to try my best to make it a smooth... whatever it is.

I open the door and am faced with his handsome, beaming face. I can't deny, it makes me happy seeing the cocky sod. He's carrying two hot drinks and a fresh bag of croissants. The scent hits my nostrils and I'm instantly hungry.

'How are we, gorgeous?'

I back up to let him step inside and swing the door shut behind him. He walks straight in to the kitchen and I end up talking to his back. 'I'm fine. Annoyed. Pissed off. Sometimes a little anxious, but other than that, I'm fine.'

He puts the drinks and food onto my worktop and turns toward me. Before I know it, I'm enveloped in him, his arms around me, and I'm hugging him back.

'I felt sick when I heard what had happened. I got a tip-off, but by the time I could do anything' – he pulls back to look me in the eye – 'you were already in hospital. I came up to see you but they were only letting family in.' He'd told me that already.

'I'm fine, honestly. Looks like I've worried them though.'

'Well you've definitely got them rattled. I think for your safety though, sweetheart, we need to start setting some ground rules while we're doing this.'

'How about taking your hands off her. That can be your first ground rule.'

I turn to see Eddie standing in the kitchen doorway, putting his T-shirt on with a sneer on his face so fucking obvious I cringe.

I needn't worry though – Tristan doesn't seem in the slightest bit perturbed, although that might not be the best reaction for Eddie.

Tristan closes in on me again, putting his arm around

me, passing me my... mmm I can smell it, piping hot English tea, and stands square, staring at Eddie.

'Now that's no way to talk to your girl's boss, is it, especially after you've got her in so much trouble. Though by the looks of it, you've got yourself into a spot of bother too. Those are some nice bruises you've got yourself there. Pissed off your own boss too, have you, Eddie? Can't say I'm surprised. I doubt they were very happy when you started shagging a journalist.'

'Hey! Watch your mouth.' I step away from him and whack him on the shoulder. 'If you two want to play this shit, throwing insults at each other, then go ahead, but keep me the fuck out of it.'

'I'm sorry, gorgeous.' He winks at me, keeping things as sweet as he can, but Eddie's far from amused.

'Her name's Jen.'

I roll my eyes and brush past him. 'I'm going to get dressed. I want to go see the mare. You're welcome to come if you like, but you both need to behave because I have neither the time nor patience for this shit.'

'You won't hear a peep out of me, other than to tell you how fantastic you look of course.' Yet another wink from Tristan, and I can see the vein on Eddie's temple begin to pulse.

'Eddie, you can come with me...' I grab his arm and drag him back toward my bedroom. 'Tristan, I'll be out in a bit, OK?'

'I'll be right here waiting for you, my love. Do hurry won't you – your croissant's getting cold, and I need to talk to you about our next move.'

I slam the bedroom door shut before Eddie can get back out there to him because he's seething, and I'd rather not see these two go at it.

'Next move? Next fucking move? You should have your feet up, recovering. That's what your next move should be.'

'Eddie, I've no idea what's going on here. I can't say I'm not anxious about your involvement in all of this, but right now I'm trusting my gut and it's telling me I can trust you, *but*, and it's a big *but*, you need to back the fuck off and let me do my job.'

'I need you to stay safe, that's what I need you to do, and doing this job' – he mimics quotation marks with his fingers – 'is just going to lead to you getting hurt.'

I put my hands on either side of his face and stand in between his legs as he perches on the end of the bed. 'You need to trust me when I say I can look after myself. I'm already looking over my shoulder, and I'll be doing that until this story is done, until they're put away. I've shown you that despite everything I've seen, everything I've heard, I'm putting my trust in you, and you need to do the same for me.'

I search his eyes for some sort of recognition that he's taken in what I'm saying, but I'm not getting anything back. Until his head falls in between my breasts and he sighs, 'Fine.'

I finish getting dressed and head into my living room, where Tristan has more than made himself at home. His shoes are off, his feet are on the table, the croissants have been put on a plate and the drinks have been poured into mugs. Mine would even appear to have had a top-up of boiling water by the looks of the steam coming off of it. He's even made a fresh tea for Eddie.

I look at him in surprise but my face instantly drops.

'I figured you two would probably be having some sort of angry shag so I thought you'd be a while. Thankfully, you thought of your wonderful breakfast-bringing guest and chose to skip it. I'm ever so grateful. As should you be. I made you a cup of tea, Eddie. I even halved my croissant for you. Perhaps now you'll stop grimacing at me?'

'Thanks.' Eddie plants himself down opposite Tristan and the tension is once again filling the room.

'You've been avoiding me for months. If I'd known that all it took was a cuppa and half a croissant, I'd have actually managed to speak with you months ago. Alas, here we are.'

'Why are you here, Tristan?' I interject before Eddie has a chance to respond. Quite frankly, I'm getting pissed off at this ridiculous display.

'We need to talk. I gather you've rattled them rather well, considering your connection to them. I had a visit from two police officers. They inform me they spoke with you too, in hospital.'

'Yes. I have a recording of it too.'

'You do?'

'Yup, Liv left her phone in there. It was set to record. I had no idea, but she got the whole thing and sent it to me. Granted, they don't exactly say much concrete stuff, but there's enough to pull them in I would assume. What I'm confused about though is that with all the evidence against them, and now with this recording, why are we not going after them?'

'Because, my love, despite the evidence as you say, which is circumstantial at best, we have no location – no idea where this is all originating from.'

'Surely someone can follow them?'

'You'd think, wouldn't you, but it seems they've got themselves well hidden, and any attempt within the police force itself to craft some kind of operation, so to speak, instantly gets squashed.'

Eddie rises from his chair and comes toward me. I'm

leaning against the door frame, but he grabs my arm and pulls me upright. He takes the tea out of my hand, kisses me on the lips and walks me to his seat, ushering me to sit down. 'So what do you propose then? Put her in further danger, just to find out where this is all coming from?'

'Well no, of course not – no one wants any harm coming to my star reporter here... you on the other hand...'

'I need you to back the fuck off. And stay away. Like I've told Jen, I need you guys to leave me alone for just a few weeks.'

'While she might fall for that shit, Eddie, I've seen you involved in this crap for far too long. I've witnessed you talking to the two gentlemen – I use the term loosely – who paid me and your loved one here a visit. You know who they are; in fact, you looked rather friendly with them, so forgive me for not trusting you or not respecting your safety enough. But, my esteemed friend, if you're as *good* as you say you are, you'll start helping us out in order to ensure Jen's safety, won't you?'

He's angry and I can't blame him, but I can't let this go either. What he's doing just isn't right. He's working with them? For them? Either way, he's involved and he shouldn't be.

'What exactly are you expecting yourself and Jen to do exactly, apart from *blow this case wide open*?' The sarcasm coming off of him is beyond a joke – after everything I've been through, he's now mocking my job, my career?

'If you're struggling to comprehend my job, my career and what it means to me, please feel free to get the fuck out, Ed.'

His response is immediate. His face drops and transforms into an expression of apology. He comes toward me, but I put my hands up, showing him I'm not happy with the way he's just spoken.

Taking hold of my wrists, he practically begs me, 'Baby, I'm sorry. I'm so sorry. I never meant for one second...' He lowers his head to make sure we have eye contact. 'I never meant for one second that your job wasn't important or of any value or worth. Please believe me. You just need to know that I've been involved with these guys for a long time and I know they have a lot of people on their side. I know what's going on; I just need to prove it. Can you trust me?'

I look away from him, pulling my hands out of his grasp. Before I can decide exactly what I think and what I want to say to him, there's another knock at the door. Only this time, Tristan gets up and buzzes them in without even checking.

'Now you two lovebirds have made up, we have work to do. Ultimately, we're looking for the location they're working out of. I don't believe for one second that the Drafter brothers, old Bert and bloody Ernie, are at the very top of this thing. Granted, I don't think they're far from the top, but correct me if I'm wrong, Eddie, there are orders coming from above them?'

Eddie sits himself back down, and as he does, he catches Tristan's eye and gives him the nod.

'If we find where this is all going on, we can stop it at the source. Let's face it, it'd be all too easy to take the Drafter brothers in and charge them for dealing drugs, but it won't stop the actual problem.'

There's a knock at my front door. Tristan reaches for the handle, but before opening the door, he lowers his voice and continues, 'They're not going to bite the hand that feeds them by ratting out the ones who are in charge. If they did, they wouldn't be alive very long in prison.'

With that, he opens the door and in steps a short guy,

clean-shaven, wearing jeans and a basic jumper. I have no idea who Tristan has just let into the flat, but I'm less concerned with who he is than why Eddie seems to have become instantly prickly. He's trying to avoid eye contact with the guy. It's so bloody obviously awkward between them that it's difficult to notice anything else.

It's not surprising either that Eddie chooses now to leave.

He kisses my forehead. 'I'll catch up with you later at some point. Stay safe for me, OK?'

'Yeah sure. Why are you suddenly leaving now though? Do you guys know each other?'

Eddie looks at him for a split second, over his shoulder, and shakes his head, but I don't believe him.

As soon as the door shuts, I turn to this total stranger who's yet to introduce himself. Despite the plain clothes, there's a badge sat on his belt and he has a distinct air or law enforcement. I'm not happy about the sudden visit, especially after my experience with two supposed policemen at the hospital, so I demand to know what's going on. 'Well? Are you going to explain what's happened or am I going to have to prise it out of you?'

'I'm not sure what you're on about?'

'Look, mate, I've already had two of your pals come visit me at the hospital...'

'They're nothing to do with me.'

'I couldn't give a fuck. You're in my home, so you best start talking now and tell me what the fuck was going on there between you and Eddie, and what's happening moving forward. I'm not your biggest fan at the moment, and considering you're on my turf, I couldn't give a fuck if you're a copper or not – you'll do as I fucking tell you to do.'

'You weren't wrong when you said she was spunky.' His eyebrow is raised as he looks at me out the side of his eye.

I peer at Tristan, who's currently beaming. His smile soon disappears when he sees my resting bitch face isn't a resting bitch face at all; I'm just bloody fuming.

'Look, gorgeous, this is Officer Clements. He's a good one, I promise. I wouldn't invite one of those morons into your home. The reason there was so much awkwardness there was for the simple fact that Eddie has been questioned by this gentleman in the past. That's all. Old Boy Wonder doesn't want you to think badly of him, which is probably why he said he didn't know him. That's all.'

'Is that true?'

'Yes, ma'am.'

'My name's Jen; I'm not a sixty-year-old woman. Less of the ma'am.'

For the next hour, Clements proceeds to get me up to speed on where we are. They know Eddie is involved and, like I suspect, he believes there's no way out for him at the moment. They're also aware of what's going on with Angel. They've had her in for questioning on multiple occasions, but she refuses to cooperate and simply says nothing's going on, despite evidence on public cameras showing her being manhandled. She simply refuses to press charges. While they could have charged her with a number of offences by now, they think she's more use on the street, pardon the pun, as she's more likely to slip up and lead them to where their operation is actually taking place.

Clements then spends the next thirty minutes discussing the actual abduction. This is the first time an officer, a genuine one I suppose, has actually asked what's happened and taken any interest.

Talking about it, I'm surprisingly calm. I think if I didn't have so much to focus on, I'd quite possibly crumble, but I'm remaining pretty strong. I explain everything that happened, including the mare, taking her and what they'd done to her. I also start telling him about his two friends meeting me and that my rather forward-thinking friend Liv managed to record them.

I pass on the recording, for which he seems eternally grateful. We spend time listening to what's said, with Tristan trying his best not to laugh at me when I give them a mouthful. He smiles at me and gives me a knowing wink. My sharp tongue obviously amuses him. I get the impression he likes a strong-willed, self-assured woman, and despite the importance of what we're doing, I can't help but think he would love Liv and all of her red-headed, fiery ways.

After what feels like an eternity of going over and over my 'ordeal' as they keep referring to it, we agree to end things there and meet again the next day.

I feel ever so slightly harassed at having to go over the details again and again, but it was necessary. Right now, however, I need to get to my horses, or as I've referred to them before on particularly stressful days, the most expensive therapy there is.

SEVEN

AS I PULL into the yard, I find Maggy's and Sarah's cars parked outside the barn. They're here. Relief rushes over me as I imagine a dirty cup of tea, sat on top of a mouse-infested box outside each stable. I want gossip. I want yard chit-chat, and I want to forget about the complications in my life.

I walk into the barn and see Zara, Sarah's mare, has already been brought in. Maggy sees me and smiles. 'Been a while since we've seen you here. How you doing, chick?'

'Not bad you know, just want to get back to normal. Where are the troublesome duo?'

'I've left Lincoln out with Scrappy. Is that OK? I'll go grab them now if you want, love?'

'No, no, let me. I'll go for a wander and get the pair in.'

'OK, love, I'll get a net ready for Lincoln. Want me to pop it outside his stable?'

'Yes please!' I say with a big cheesy grin.

Before I grab their headcollars, I walk past them toward Hattie's stable where she's happily munching away. She notices me and slowly wanders over to the front of the stable. I get the impression she recognises me. I didn't think she would after I practically abandoned her. She looks in a much better state, if only for the new rug she has on, keeping her warm, and the huge fresh bed, along with a full haynet and a fresh bucket of water.

'We'll see how you get on, shall we, madam, and then perhaps start introducing the haylage. You could do with the calories. I'll sort out some feed for you in a minute. Little and often. But I've gotta get the big lad in first.'

I look over the door and see a few piles in there where she's been in through the day. I could walk out and grab Lincoln and do her later or I could quickly grab them now while it's quiet in here. I decide the latter is the better option and quickly grab a bucket and shavings fork.

I open her door slowly and walk in as quietly as I can. She watches me as she backs up, putting a little more space between us. She's unhappy about the shavings fork. In fact, I'd say she's petrified of the shavings fork – to the point her eyes are on stalks and she's very clearly giving me a warning with her ears back. She's shot into the corner and now turned her side to me. She's giving me ample warning that she's unhappy with what I'm doing.

I decide that it's best to drop the fork, and as soon as I do, she softens a little. I grab some rubber gloves from just outside the door and start picking up her droppings by hand.

Now, she's a totally different horse. She starts inspecting what I'm doing, sniffing in the bucket, sniffing the back of my hair and even following me around the stable. She's clearly been beaten with the fork at some point. That's definitely where she draws the line, but that's fine. I'm happy to take it slowly with that, getting her used to it. That we can overcome.

I rise up and pat her gently, scratching her shoulder, and she responds by attempting to very gently groom me back. It's very sweet, and it's a monumental occasion.

As I make my way out of the stable, I see Maggy and Sarah have stopped what they're doing to watch. Maggy has a tear in her eye, and Sarah has her hands together, mouthing a very quiet 'yay' to me as I shut the door behind me.

What a huge step for her. While it might be nothing to everyone else, it's huge for her. I couldn't be prouder of her.

I make my way to Lincoln's boxes and grab a treat from his drawer. She's waiting for it too; she knows what I'm bringing her. I cannot wipe the smile from my face as I check over her door to make sure she has enough hay to last her the night, along with water. Her bed is huge too. There's no chance she won't be comfy on there. I'd be more than happy to sleep on that myself; in fact with the tiredness beginning to take over, it's actually rather tempting.

I walk back past Lincoln's stable and grab his headcollar, grabbing Scrappy's as I head to the open end of the barn. I swing around and see Maggy tidying up outside of her stable. 'I'll finish him off tonight. It's starting to get dark. Make your way home and I'll make sure he's tucked up, in bed and happy.'

'You sure? I don't want to be leaning on you too much after everything you've been through.'

I instinctively roll my eyes at her but do so with a cheeky grin so she knows I'm still appreciative of her being so concerned about me. 'I'm fine, I promise. Let me sort him out. You too, Sarah; I'll turn all the lights off and lock up the feed-room door at the back. Go plop yourselves on your sofa and have a nice evening, guys.'

I'm waving them goodbye over my shoulder as I make

my way toward the field to get the boys, the last two out as usual.

They're standing by the gate. It's by no means dark, but you can see that the sun is starting to set which to them means it's time to come in, get comfy and get some dinner in their bellies. Lincoln is standing politely behind Scrappy, who is, without a doubt, in charge. It's a mixed herd that they're in and they love it, but these two are thick as thieves.

Lincoln moves alongside Scrappy and puts his head over the gate as I approach, and his headcollar goes on nice and quickly. Scrappy starts nickering at me, almost as if he's trying to hurry me up, and I happily oblige, leaning over the gate and popping his headcollar on too. I daren't open the gate to do it. He's known at the yard for being a total pain in the backside, and as soon as that latch goes, if he hasn't got a headcollar on, the fucker is off.

With them both secured, I open the gate and let Tiny Legs shoot out on his own first. He comes to an abrupt halt when he reaches the end of the lead rope and turns around, waiting for Lincoln to make his way out.

They both turn, knowing the routine – I have to close the gate behind me.

When the click of the gate's latch sounds once more, I turn around and start walking back to the barn, only this time, Scrappy has other ideas and decides to buck out at me and fuck off up the lane. Little bastard. I have no gloves on so let go as the rope burns through my hand.

'You little shit!' Bastard animals. No wonder they're nicknamed Shitlands. Absolute fucker of an animal, and I curse his name all the way back to the barn, where I know he'll be, desperately trying to get into his stable to eat his handful of feed. It's more like a peace offering than anything else. He doesn't need any hard feed, but Maggy feels rotten for not giving him anything so he gets a handful of nuts. I think it's to make her feel better more than anything.

As I arrive at the barn, I see his stable door closing and notice the person who's doing it. Eddie is the last person I want to see right now. I wanted to be here, to escape. To be around Lincoln, Hattie, even Scrappy for fuck's sake. I wanted the peace and quiet of the barn.

As I walk past Scrappy's stable door, I push the kick bolt across with my foot and call him a wanker over his door, then give the ungrateful sod a quick scratch on his forehead, trying my best to ignore Eddie, although he's pretty hard to miss.

'Are you going to ignore me or will you talk to me eventually? I thought we were OK this morning?'

I sigh outwardly. I just don't want this.

'I don't have the energy for this, Ed.'

I carry on with Lincoln and tie him up outside his stable, unbuckling the surcingles on his rug and then the leg straps at the back. I give them a shake when they don't immediately untangle and make my way to the front to start unfastening his neck straps as Eddie pulls a chair up next to where Lincoln's tied up. He's watching me as I undo the straps across his chest. The rug is soaked, so I carry it into the feed room and hang it up on one of the hooks to dry.

I come back out and give Lincoln a quick brush off. Eddie silently passes me the hoof pick, anticipating what I need next, and gets up to hold the bucket under his feet each time I pick them out. We're both silent, neither of us wanting to talk. Me because I can't and won't handle it right now; him perhaps because he knows how I'm feeling.

I grab the stable rug that's hanging over the door and throw it over Lincoln, then start doing his chest straps up as

Eddie walks round to fasten his back-leg straps. I pull the neck of the rug forward and close the straps there as Ed bends down to buckle the surcingles below.

Lincoln's hay has been put down already thanks to the girls, and his bed is ready for him to pop straight in. His water's fresh. He just needs a feed. I watch as Eddie does the last belly strap, and then I unclip his lead rope from the headcollar, walking him back a few steps before leading him into his stable.

I leave the leap rope dangling, ready for me to simply clip straight on in the morning, remove his headcollar, grab the waiting feed buckets and head for the feed room. I bend down mid stride as I pass Hattie's stall and grab her buckets as well, Eddie following behind me.

The metal feed bin was such a big outlay when I first got Lincoln but has been with me for years. It's dirty, dusty and dented in numerous areas, but it's fantastic. Stores a whole winter's worth of feed in it. Even with Hattie now needing fed, it still has more than enough for the pair of them. I have her on exactly the same as I have Lincoln on: nuts, chaff and some garlic and oil. Simple feed. If she needs an extra boost soon, I might add in some barely for her. I much prefer feeding straight feed like that rather than those mixes from the local feed store. They always seem to have a plethora of ingredients in that you never quite know the purpose of.

I throw all four buckets down on the floor near the feed bin and start filling them up.

'How much has Hattie been having?' I look up at Eddie as I ask him, and he's almost taken aback that I'm actually talking to him.

'Umm, I'd say she's on a little less than Lincoln now maybe. Not quite the same as him but certainly not far off.'

I make her feeds up per his instructions and then dampen them all down. That's one for each of them tonight and one for tomorrow. I pop a feed-bucket cover on two of them. I had to borrow one from Sarah as I only ever had the one for Lincoln. I'll need to grab a few bits for Hattie actually. I think she's going to cost me a pretty penny, and not just in money either. She's going to need a lot of time. Do I have the time to give her? That's the question.

I lower them each a feed over the door and leave the other two outside, ready for the morning, then go to start sweeping up, but I'm stopped when a plate-sized hand wraps around my own. 'Stop, Jen – just stop. For fuck's sake, enough. Talk to me. Please?'

I rip my hand from his and huff as I storm past him. He has a fucking nerve. I'm meant to be getting a break from this crap. I'm meant to be getting to grips with everything, even recovering from the sodding 'ordeal' or whatever everyone's calling it now and he just won't leave me alone. When is he going to leave me alone?

I scoop up a couple of loose haynets outside the stables and decide to make up some nets ready for the morning.

'Just stop, Jen! Enough. You have to talk to me sometime. Did that copper say something this morning?'

'How do you know he was a copper?'

Eddie stops in his tracks. I turn and see the distinct expression of a rabbit caught in the headlights. He's been caught and he's not happy about it.

'So you knew him then?'

'What did he say? Tell me what he said.'

'It doesn't matter what he said. You know him? Are you involved with the Drafter brothers more than you're letting on?'

'Not this again, surely? Why do you keep doing this? Why won't you just trust me?'

'Because you're making it really bloody hard.'

He rounds in front of me, taking the haynets out of my hand. I've been attacking the nets, angrily stuffing them with hay as I speak to him. He brings it out in me, making me more and more angry with every sentence spoken.

'Do you want to be with me? Because I want to be with you.'

'It's not that simple, Eddie – you know that.'

'Then let's make it that simple. Do you love me?'

'Jesus Christ, Ed, steady on. Do you really think it's a good idea asking those sorts of questions right now?'

'Do you love me, Jen? Because I know without question that I'm in love with you.'

I feel my mouth drop. I can't believe what I'm hearing – so much so that I ask him to say it again.

'Jen Seaton, I'm in love with you, and regardless of what's going on, I want to be with you. I'm so fucking scared that I'm going to lose you over all this shit.'

I want to answer. I want to tell him that I think I'm falling for him, but right now not only is my mind far too confused with what's happening around me, but I'm just dumbfounded that those words have left his mouth. He's in love with me. I'm frozen to the spot, just staring at him.

'Have I gone too far? Have I freaked you out now? Please don't say I've freaked you out!'

He watches me for a moment longer, just staring back at him, open-mouthed before he throws caution to the wind completely. 'Oh fuck it.'

His hands are on either side of my face, cupping my cheeks as he attacks my mouth. My hands fly up around his shoulders of their own accord, grabbing on to him as quickly as they possibly can.

As soon as my arms have hooked on to him, he's moving his hands down to my arse with lightning speed, grabbing each cheek and lifting me from the ground with force. As if they've been given an immediate order, my legs wrap themselves around his waist. He's carrying me, kissing me hard and deep as he walks us both over to the metal feed bins. He wants me as much as I want him right now and there's just no stopping it.

He lowers me onto the feed bin, his mouth refusing to leave my lips. His hands remain firm on my backside. I'm wearing my tracksuit bottoms, the least sexy item in my wardrobe, along with an oversized zip-up. He wastes no time in ripping the zip down and pushing it off my shoulders, all the while attacking my mouth and taking everything I have for himself. My scrappy top underneath does nothing to cover my breasts, much to his delight as he simply pulls it down. I throw my head back in sheer pleasure as his hands get to work on my nipples.

Then, as quickly as it started, it stops. He backs off, panting, leaving me breathless, quickly hurrying to cover up.

'What the hell?'

'I don't want us getting caught.'

'What? There's no one here.'

'Just be quiet.'

He takes my hand, helps me off of the feed bin and, without breaking eye contact, slowly but surely backs toward the feed-room door. As he reaches it, with me about a metre behind him, he leans back and looks out of the door to check if we're alone. By the wicked grin on his face, I'd say we are.

With everything that's going on, I should be running. I should be telling him I want nothing to do with him, yet here I am. My heart is racing with excitement and I can't wipe the smile from my face.

He leans back and shuts the door, moving a random, dusty old chair underneath the door handle with one hand while he keeps hold of me with the other.

As he lets go of the chair, he brings his hand around and adjusts himself. He's hard. Though I'm not surprised because I'm already so fucking wet it's unreal. He looks me up and down, like I'm an animal he's hunting and claiming as his own. I could not want him more right now if I tried. All the anger, the fury – it's all gone, and it's been replaced with a desire so strong that I'm about to fuck him senseless in the feed room at the barn.

Uptight Jen has well and truly done a disappearing act. I'm not sure where this side of me has come from, but I'm running with it, and him for that matter.

I decide to take charge, pulling him toward me. He needs no more instructions as he sinks his lips onto mine and invades my mouth once more with his. My hands come up, gripping onto his hair so tight I think I might rip great big chunks from his head, but he doesn't care. He's too busy undoing the string at the top of my tracksuit bottoms.

During my many years of fantasising about us finally getting together, never did I imagine myself in a horse-shit-stained tracksuit.

I envisaged lacy underwear, skintight clothing that gave him just enough of a hint of what he could find underneath. My hair would be perfectly coiffed and shining. More importantly, we would have been on freshly laid sheets, in a decadent bedroom somewhere. We were never in the mouse trap that is our feed room, and I most certainly wasn't dressed like a builder who's yet to have a shower after a hard day's work.

Yet here we are. He looks hassled and I just look like a soap dodger – and neither one of us cares one bit. We're far too concerned with each other. This is so much better than I could have ever fantasised about.

While my mind is doing somersaults, I fail to notice that he's unhooked my bra and pulled it down below my breasts. They're out for him to enjoy, and fuck me do I want him to enjoy them.

Before lifting me up, he pulls my tracksuit bottoms down as far as they'll go. He plays with the waistline of my knickers, but instead of pulling them down, he leaves them where they are, mumbling, 'They can stay,' as he puts me straight back onto the feed bin. I grapple with his waistband and pull his zip down over the hard bulge that's formed below his jeans.

As I unzip and reveal his boxers, I stop kissing him and take a moment to slowly and gently lower the waistband of his boxers. I want his cock, all of him, inside me, but first, I want him in my mouth.

I jump down, turn him around and push him back so he's leaning against the metal, then lower myself to my knees. I lick the end of his cock so gently, yet it obviously sends waves of electricity up his shaft as he throws his head back, hissing at the effect it has on him.

I grab hold of his cock and put him inside of me. I'm full. His long, thick shaft is barely inside of me before he hits the back of my throat and there's still more to go. I suck hard and then gently run my teeth along the shaft. He's unravelling before me, and I'm loving every second of being in control. I start pumping with my hand as my mouth shoots up and down, sucking, biting, devouring him, but he grabs me soon after to stop. 'Stop. Stop now. Fuck me, you're going to send me over the edge.'

I stand up, wipe my mouth of the pre-cum that's all over me, worried he won't want to kiss me, but he doesn't care. His kiss is forceful, almost violent. It's like he's angry at everything that's happening around us and he's taking it out on my mouth. I'm not objecting though. I want more of it.

He spins me round, lifts up my right leg and angles his body so his cock can find my entrance. After a little manoeuvring, he's in and fucking me so hard, I can feel the metal digging into my lower back. I don't care though because he's hitting the sweet spot, smashing into my clit with every thrust.

The faster and harder he goes, the more I start to build, and before I can give him any warning, I cum, quicker than I thought possible with penetrative sex. He follows swiftly after, giving me a few more thrusts for good measure after he's done so. And there we lean against the metal feed bin, holding each other as his dick softens and falls out of me.

We don't say much. It feels like we've said everything we need to say with sex. I feel more of him start to drip out of me, so grab my knickers and adjust them so they're back covering me, then pull my trousers up and, oddly enough, turn away from him while I tie the string. I have no idea why but I do.

They never show this bit in movies, do they? You never see her clearing up the spunk after they've shagged. It just seems to magically disappear up her vagina, never to be seen again. They also tend to lie there in post-coital bliss, neither one peeing. Asking for a UTI.

I turn around and catch his eye. 'I need to go to the bathroom.'

'Well obviously – you have spunk dripping out of you.'

I giggle. In spite of what's happening, it's moments like this that take me away and remind me of the relationship we had before all of this. The connection is still very much there, and I miss it.

I head to the bathroom, clean myself up as best I can and then come back to the barn to find him sitting outside Hattie's stable, quietly and patiently, just letting her sniff as and when she wants. He's being so gentle with her. A stark contrast to how he was fucking me just moments ago. I love that I get to see both sides of him, but then there's that other side. The side I wish wasn't real.

He spots me watching him and smiles. 'She's getting there, isn't she? She's starting to come round. Talking of coming round, can I come back to yours tonight?'

'Please don't take this the wrong way...'

'Well I fucking will now you've said that.' He rolls his eyes and looks away for a moment before looking straight back at me. 'Let me guess, you need space or some shit?'

'Something like that. You don't hate me, do you?'

He looks almost hurt at my question, but I'm not going to apologise for wanting my space. For not being comfortable with who he is and what he's currently doing, but I do feel bad for fucking him and then telling him to leave me alone. I know I'm giving major mixed signals, but right now, I just need the space.

'I could never hate you. Never. Please don't ever ask me that again.'

He turns and grabs his jacket, which is slung over a spare stable door, and kisses me on the cheek. He wraps one hand around my waist while the other one holds his coat, dangling by his side, and leans down to get into my field of vision. 'I'll give you space tonight, but I can't promise that I'll stay away from you tomorrow.'

He winks at me and kisses me once more on the lips, lingering just a little longer, to remind me of what I'm missing tonight. It's so hard telling him that I don't want to spend the night with him when I bloody well do. Jesus Christ, the things I could do to him tonight...

Despite my once again burning desires, I remind myself that I have people to see tonight, namely my favourite redhead, and I need her words of wisdom more than ever. I finish our lingering kiss to stop it from becoming something else and squeeze his arm before walking off to lock the feed room. I hear him walking back to his truck as I do.

I say goodnight to Hattie first before heading to my boy; Lincoln leans over only briefly as he's far too busy munching on his hay now. I do my checks on each of them: hay, water, nice bed and feed, and then make my way out to the car, switching off the lights at the end of the barn as I do.

'Goodnight,' echoes from me as I shout it over my shoulder, unlocking my car as I step toward it. The indicator lights flash as it unlocks, lighting up the whole yard, and I see Eddie sitting in his truck. He's waiting for me, making sure I get in my car and on my way home safe.

Bloody hell, I think I'm in love with him.

EIGHT

I GIVE Liv a text before I set off to tell her I'm on my way home and give Eddie a small wave as I shoot off in front of him. My phone lights up while I'm driving through the country lanes, but I ignore it. It's most likely just Liv telling me she'll be at mine in ten or something. No point checking it while I'm driving – I'd rather wait the five minutes and keep my eyes on the road.

As I pull up at the kerb, I park in my usual space before grabbing my phone. As suspected, there's a message from Liv.

LIV: I'll be at yours in ten, sweet cheeks.

But there are three other messages too. I read them one by one.

Tristan: I'm coming to yours. Got some info from that Clements.

Mum: Are you OK, love? How's your day been? x

Eddie: I don't care if it's too much, I love you, Jen xx

The last message takes my breath away somewhat. I want to shout it from the rooftops and let him know I feel exactly the same way, but now just isn't the time. The last thing I need are more feelings. More reason to be biased toward him with all this going on around me.

I text Mum back quickly.

Jen: All good, been working all day and just finished at the horses. Hattie's coming along, starting to trust a little more, and Lincoln is as gorgeous as ever. Will buzz you tomorrow xx

Then I jump out the car and shout at the stunning redhead I see exiting a funky red hatchback. The car's as fiery as her hair. It suits her down to the ground. A funky Audi A3 with jet-black leather interior and a sound system that, up until thirty seconds ago, was benefiting all of my neighbours.

'Hey you!'

'Heeeyyyyy!' She's as excited to see me as I am her.

'Quick, let's get upstairs. Tristan is coming round. Reckons he's got more info on the case. Did you grab a bottle?'

She lifts two bottles from her bag with a deadpan face, 'Don't ask stupid questions, Jen.'

'Fair enough,' I say, giggling at her as she saunters through the security door once I've opened it with my fob and we make our way upstairs.

As much as I'd love a shower, I suspect I don't have time so I quickly change my clothes and give myself a quick spruce in bathroom. Anything to get rid of the smell of sex. It's all that's filling my nostrils.

I change into yet more loungewear, only this time it's far more acceptable. I bought it cheap online, but it looks less stables, more casual wear for home. It doesn't stink of horse piss either, which is always a bonus when it comes to my wardrobe.

By the time I've walked into the living room, Liv has

poured out two glasses of wine, and I'm just about to sit on the sofa when the security buzzer goes. I glance quickly out of my window and see Tristan waiting at the entrance before buzzing him up.

'I'm sorry about this, Liv; it shouldn't be long.'

'Honey, do what you need to do. We've got all night to get plastered and enjoy ourselves.'

I open the door and find myself having timed it perfectly. Tristan's hand is raised, ready to knock. I've never seen him caught off guard before. It's quite funny actually.

'Must you do things like that, gorgeous?'

'Yes, always. So, what have you got to tell me?'

'Oh bloody hell, straight to the point then? No, hi, Tristan, how are you, you handsome rogue?'

'No. What have you got to tell me?'

I walk into the living room, glass of wine in hand, and attempt to introduce him before Liv reminds me they've met before. That's not what shocks me though. It's the familiarity there seems to be between the two of them, and the obvious flirtation. What the hell's going on there?

'Glass of wine, Tris?'

'Ah, no thank you, gorgeous. I'm driving. I just wanted to come here and let you know that Angel's been taken in for questioning.'

'Again? Clements said they've done that multiple times and it never unearths anything. What's it going to do this time apart from perhaps anger her into abducting me again?'

'Honey, you're safe.'

Liv rubs my hands and backs up Tristan's reassurance with a wink and a gentle squeeze. I must be looking a little more anxious at the thought of going through that again than I realised.

'Well actually, it would seem she's let something slip.'

'Oh my God, you're kidding? Finally! What's she said?'

'Ooh yeah, what's the little whore-bag gone and said?'

I look at Liv. She's so involved and so deadly protective of me. I know she'd love five minutes alone with Angel to show her what she really thinks of her. She's loyal to the end, and I couldn't be more grateful to call her my best friend.

I tear myself away from admiring my favourite redhead to catch the tail end of what Tristan is saying. 'Sorry, say that again – something about underground?'

'Pay attention, gorgeous. She said, and I quote, "they'll never find it; it's too far down". Then apparently she rather quickly corrected herself and said "too far around". God love her for trying, but she's thick as shit, isn't she?'

'So we're looking for an underground location for this hot mess?'

'Yup! What's more of a breakthrough is that today was the first time she didn't deny something was happening. Whenever the drugs were mentioned, or her being pimped out' – he looks at Liv with a sad expression – 'poor cow' – before returning his attention to me – 'she never denied it. Just said they'll never find any evidence.

'She might have also said that Eddie was involved quite heavily, etc. If your golden boy is doing his best to sort things, as he says, it looks like Angel's turned on him. I'm guessing it's one of those "if I'm going down, everyone's going down" attitudes.'

'Shit, this is huge. So all we need to do now is start looking underground?'

Liv snorts into her wine. 'Alright, Danger Mouse. What are you going to do, start fucking burrowing tomorrow at first light?'

They both start cackling at my expense, though I can't say I blame them. It was a bit of a clanger. I give in to the feeling and collapse on my sofa, laughing far too much, before showing Tristan my empty glass. I've been taking sips, or gulps should I say, without even realising it.

Being the absolute gentleman that he is, he walks forward and fills my glass. He does the same with Liv, only this time, their eye contact lingers just a smidge too long. There's definitely something there. My goodness, they must have had more than a brief chit-chat at the hospital.

After pouring us our wine, Tristan makes his excuses and heads out. I'm guessing he's on his way home, but with his work ethic, I wouldn't be surprised if he were heading back to the office to put some more hours in.

Liv and I spend the rest of the evening chit-chatting about random shit. She has the ability to take me away from everything that's going on with ease. She also happens to mention, on multiple occasions in her drunken state, that Tristan is fit and, quote, 'fuckable'. I try my best to make a mental note to talk to her more when we're sober so I can really gauge what she's thinking, though I can't deny with the state I'm currently in, I may not have a clue about it in the morning.

Somewhere between midnight and 1 a.m., we end up both crashing in my bed. Despite the amount of wine we've consumed, and the distinct lack of food –because, as Liv says, 'eating's cheating' – we still manage to find two sets of clean pyjamas and wish each other sweet dreams before collapsing in a pile on my bed.

I don't know what I'd do without Liv and her fiery ways, guaranteed to make me smile all the time. She's always just what I need, and she knows it too. Always with me, at a moment's notice. This girl sees me through thick and thin, and I wouldn't want to be without her.

NINE

AS I OPEN MY EYES, I have to blink a few times to make the view in front of me come into focus. It's a mug, a few inches from my face.

'Drink it. You won't feel like shit if you do.'

'How do you know I feel like shit?' I roll over on my side and do my best to stop the thumping in my head by delicately laying it on a doubled-up pillow.

'Get up and bloody well drink it. You've got work today and so have I. Hurry the fuck up. I haven't got all day, treacle tits.'

I take her orders and down whatever hideous shite she's put in the mug. She's right though, it does make me feel better. I start to feel almost normal after I manage to get a slice of toast inside of me, swiftly followed by a shower.

Within thirty minutes, I'm at the paper, walking up the internal stairs. I'm glad to get a text from Maggy, telling me her Shitland of a pony apologises for his shameful behaviour the night before and she's just popped him out with Lincoln. She's also skipped out Hattie, refreshed her water and given her fresh hay and a small feed. I smile to myself at how lucky I am to have such amazing friends in my life and head into the main office space, heading straight toward Tristan's office.

Officer Clements is already there and, by the looks of it, filling in Tristan on some more news. '... basically just a matter of finding what would otherwise be disused under-ground sub stations, train stations perhaps? It could be anywhere. Literally anywhere.'

Tristan catches my eye and ushers me in.

'Hey, guys. Any news this morning?'

'Hey, gorgeous.' He winks and gives me that usual smile of his, before he continues. 'Officer Clements is just giving me an update. Basically, as soon as we find the location, that's pretty much it. They'll be able to carry out all neces-sary arrests and you, my little love, can sink your teeth into putting this story together.' He's happy, but I can see he's nervous at the same time.

'What's wrong? You don't look as happy as I thought you would?'

'I'm just worried. I'm worried in case we find out Eddie has a little more to do with it than you, sorry, we currently believe. I don't think I could bear to see the disappointment on your face. I'm not great at helping mend broken hearts.'

He gives me what I think is supposed to be a comforting squeeze on the shoulder, but surprisingly enough, I'm feeling pretty confident in Eddie. I don't know what's changed overnight, but I'm feeling slightly brighter than I was yesterday. It has absolutely nothing to do with the immense orgasm I had at the yard last night – or the fact he told me he was in love with me. I'm not that easily swayed, I'm certain of it. Mostly certainly... pretty sure.

The decision is made, while I'm staring out the window battling with my own thoughts, to revisit the scene where I was found after my abduction. They want me to see if I recognise anything. If anything jogs my memory. While it's not my favourite place in the world, I'm not hugely bothered about heading back there.

I agree to their request and find myself being thanked hugely by good old Officer Clements. He's definitely very calculated with regards to how he speaks to me now. I can only imagine he wasn't too impressed with my sharp tongue before and has actively avoided encouraging a reoccurrence.

Luckily for my beat-up little car, we're escorted to the old half empty yard in his police vehicle, or the jam sandwich as my mum sometimes used to call them. I have no idea why though? Perhaps the older 'bobby cars', as I've heard her say, had different signage on.

My mind drifts away in the back of the car throughout the journey. I think of everything, from Eddie and our amazing sex in the feed barn to the undeniable connection between Liv and Tristan. I wonder if either recognise the attraction from the other? I wonder if I'll have to set them up? Though that could prove awkward if things went south and I had to spend time with both after a shitty break-up. Maybe that wouldn't be such a good idea.

My worried thoughts about their imaginary break-up are thankfully disturbed before they can go too far by the car coming to a halt. The car jolts a little as Clements whacks the handbrake on before it's fully stopped, and as it does, I find myself faced with the place I suddenly hate the most. I didn't feel like this last time, but looking at it in the cold light of day just makes me sick.

It's much bigger than I remember too.

It's totally empty. Clements informs us that since they found me here, at the very place he's stopped, the Drafter brothers have cleared out. It's now empty, disused, but all I can think is that they didn't find me. Eddie did. Instead of being the pedantic journo in the back of the car however, I keep my mouth shut and simply nod.

I place my hand on the door handle, and before I open it completely, I remind myself that not only is this place completely empty but I'm here with two men, one of whom is a law enforcement officer. I'm in safe hands.

I unlock the car door, but before I can step foot outside, Tristan is out and in front of me in seconds. He takes my hand, without asking, and wraps his arm around my shoulders.

It's funny how he can transition from the sarcastic, overly flirty bloke I work with to a truly caring... well, friend really. I guess he's more than just a colleague now. We're both involved in something rather serious, and it feels like there's no way out until we both make sure it's over.

I wander through the gate, leaving Tristan to trail behind me. He still has hold of my hand, but he's walking directly behind me now.

I take it all in, walking past the old disused office where I managed to find a computer to send out my location.

I keep going and find myself at Hattie's stable. The bed is still there. Still covered in shit and piss. The water bucket still empty; the door still swinging open.

Another step or two forward and we come face to face with the stable where I woke up. I lean on the door and look inside. I hate it here. I want to leave.

This time round feels different, and I'm not comfortable being here. Tristan must sense my unease as he closes the gap between us, standing directly behind me as he brings his arms up and wraps them both around my shoulders. He's so tall that his chin sits conveniently on top of my head.

'Alright, gorgeous? Feeling OK?'

'Yeah, it just feels more real today, you know?'

'Yeah, I get that. Nothing you recognise?'

'No.' And my voice wanders off as I walk out of his bear hug and into the stable. I run my hands along the dividing wall that separated Hattie and I, then cast my gaze all around the space before coming to the stable door and leaning on it, looking out.

Clements is looking around, venturing over into their office. I remember looking out of the stable door and seeing them in there. I remember it being lit up. There was Angel, and one or two other men. I can't remember fully. I do remember being scared though. I never want to feel like that again.

I look up, into the distance, and see the thing that confused me. Is it a water tower or a windmill? Whatever it is, it just brings back way too many memories. Memories I don't want.

'I'm done, Tristan; I've had enough. I don't want to be here. I can't be here. I need to go.'

I look up at him with pleading eyes and he gets it. Straight away he's shouting, 'Clements, time to go now, matey.'

He takes my hand, leads me out the stable door and starts walking me toward the police car. He opens the back door for me to slide in, only this time he gets in with me, keeping hold of my hand. He's sat on my left, holding my left hand with his as he wraps his long right arm around me. He lifts his arm a little so I can plug the seat belt in and puts it back as soon as he hears the click.

I want to go now. I'm done.

TEN

I'M in a complete state and need to calm myself, but for some reason, my flat just isn't doing it at the minute. This is usually my little sanctuary, but right now, I don't feel secure. I don't want to be on my own.

I've had a number of calls on this new phone, but the damn thing has gone to silent so I've missed every single one. Stupid fucking phone. Not that it matters. I don't have the energy to call people back. So I do exactly what I know will make me feel better. I throw on my leggings, a hoodie and my wellies, and head out.

Visiting that yard today has unnerved me. I don't feel good at all, so I need to be somewhere that makes me feel instantly calm and there's only one place that does that. Lincoln's yard.

Technically there's nothing there for me to do, as Maggy's sorting him and Hattie for me today, but it's the stables – there's always something I can find that needs doing. Even if it's just sitting on the mice-infested, dusty box outside to gossip and whine. I need this. I need to just relax and keep myself busy. If I'm not feeling sick and constantly worrying about what happened and what might have happened, I'm thinking way too much about where this potential location could be. My mind, and body, needs to calm. I need to relax and chill out as best I can.

I pull up at the yard and find it's empty, so I jump out of the car and race to the barn entrance, turning the lights on. It instantly makes me feel safer. I suddenly don't like the darkness today. I need light all around me.

Something doesn't feel quite right though. They're on edge, all of them.

I come to Zara first. She's looking off into the distance and then circling her stable, Scrappy is standing at the back of the stable and Lincoln, Mr Steady Eddie, is box walking like there's no tomorrow. The neck on his rug is also flying open around him; the straps haven't been done up. That's odd. Maggy is meticulous about that stuff.

Are the others getting stressed because Lincoln is stressed? Though an open neck wouldn't normally bother him.

I don't understand what's got him all riled up until I look past him and see that Hattie is thick with sweat. She's shaking and walking backward and forward, weaving and then box walking, before repeating the whole process again. She's petrified. Her rug isn't on and she's covered in thick white foam. She's dripping. What the fuck is going on? This isn't right.

I walk toward her stable, but she goes crazy. There's no way I can get near her right now. I look over her stable door and see the rug on the floor. It's covered in droppings and has been walked all over. It's trashed. I look up at her head and see a mark under her eye. Her eye is swollen too and there's a chunk of mane out of her neck.

I step back, suddenly very aware of what's going on. How could I not think they'd come here?

I turn and run toward Lincoln's stable, seeing a chunk of hair on the floor outside. I also notice my drawers open. How did I not see that before? My junk drawers are open and the scissors are on top of them. It's a message. They want me to know they've been here.

I go into Lincoln's stable and check his neck. Just as I thought there would be, there's a huge chunk of mane missing. That's why they're all on edge. The Drafter brothers have been here.

I pick my phone out of my pocket and, doing my best to control my breathing, dial Eddie. He picks up after one ring and I sob down the phone, 'They've been here. They've fucking been here and been near the horses.'

'I'm on my way. Just stay where you are, OK?'

I nod, even though he isn't able to see my response, and hang up. I feel sick. So I ring the only other person I know who can help.

The phone rings only twice before she picks up. 'Alice?'

There's a second or two of silence before she speaks. Given how far away she is, it's not as instant as a UK phone call.

'Hey, you! What's wrong? You sound weird.'

'You know you have your two horses in that spare field. Do you think there's room for another two? I need to put Lincoln and Hattie somewhere quick. I don't have time to explain. I just need them out, somewhere safe. Can I throw them in there?'

'Jen, do what you want. My two are on ten acres of lush grazing. There's more than enough room, but what's going on? And who the fuck is Hattie? Is everything OK?'

'Alice, I promise I'll explain everything when I see you. I just need to get them away from the barn.'

The sense of relief that washes over me is immense. I'll get them out of here and away from where Angel knows they are. If she didn't attack them herself, she undoubtedly led whoever did here, so I need them away – fast.

'How's the States? You met a hunky cowboy and rode off into the sunset yet?'

'Ha! Well it's funny you should say that, but it's a bit of a long story so I'll fill you in when you sound less hassled. Besides, I've gotta be out on a trail ride in like five minutes. Whack Lincoln and this Hattie out with my two. It's no worries. You know the code to the key safe, right?'

'Yup, your birthday. I've got it.'

'OK, babe, stay safe, and I hope everything's OK. We'll speak soon, alright?'

'Yup, catch you soon, Alice, and thank you.'

I hang up and run to the feed room, and immediately start rummaging in Sarah's things, grab the key to her trailer and make my way out back down the barn as I see Eddie's truck pulling in.

I give Zara and Scrappy a check, noting they're back to being pretty calm. I can't see any mane taken from them; in fact I don't even think their stable doors have been opened. This was quite clearly a message directed at me, to warn me. I wonder if they know we paid a visit to the old yard today. There's got to be something there. Something hidden in plain sight that we're getting too close to?

Eddie jumps out of the truck and runs in. I throw the keys to the trailer at him. I don't have time to tell Sarah I'm using her trailer; she'll understand.

'Unlock the trailer and hitch it up to the truck. I'm taking Linc and Hattie to Alice's field.'

'Alice is in the States isn't she?'

'Yeah, but she said it's fine. There's plenty of room so get it ready. I'm going to rug these two up in turnouts and we'll load them straight up.'

I grab Lincoln's medium-weight turnout and throw it on him in his stable. Now time to try the same with Hattie, who, right now, I don't think wants me anywhere near her.

I grab a turnout rug that I've been borrowing from Zara and place it gently over her stable door, but before I can go in and get her, Eddie pushes me aside.

'You're not going in when she's in that state. Let me get her.'

She still has a headcollar on, to make things nice and easy for Maggy or anyone else doing her for me. Unfortunately, it's one of those easy-break ones, and just as Eddie grabs it, she backs away and it virtually falls apart.

I tell him to leave. I think he considers refusing, but he must see my face and he instantly does as I've asked. She's fine with me; she just needs to remember that.

I stand in the doorway of her stable and make my body as soft as possible. I look down at the floor, closing my arms inward, and stand with one heel cocked so it's off the floor, doing my utmost to appear relaxed and calm.

She slowly responds. Her pacing and giraffe-like neck begin to lessen and she starts to ease off. She comes toward me, sniffing me, but she's still very much on edge. I slowly put one of Lincoln's spare headcollars over her muzzle, talking to her gently as I do, and manage to get it over one ear before she backs off.

'Fuck's sake, that's going to come off if I can't whip it over the other ear.'

Eddie steps forward and starts gently rubbing her chest, moving his hand up to her shoulders and onto her neck.

She's surprisingly relaxed around him and actually lets him move the headcollar over the other ear, though it's not without a big fuss.

As soon as it's over both ears, I click the strap under her jaw and attach the lead rope, bringing her out of the stable. I then hold on as Eddie very slowly places the rug on her. It's a painfully slow process, as we try to be as gentle and calm as we possibly can.

There's a real fine line when it comes to stuff like this. You don't want to be too slow and cautious, as that can often make them worse, but at the same time, we're not able to just throw the rug on her like we would Lincoln. Together, however, we're getting it done. She's actually OK with the leg straps too, which is a nice surprise.

I have no idea how I'm going to change her rug when she's in that huge ten-acre field, but right now, I don't care. I just want her and Lincoln out of here, and I want them out of here now.

Eddie gives me the nod to say the trailer is ready and I hand him Hattie, then run to Lincoln and take him straight toward the trailer. Like the pro that he is, he walks straight on, despite what he's been through while I wasn't here. I load him in the offside of the trailer as he's clearly the heavier of the two, then turn around and take Hattie from Eddie. 'Can you go grab two haynets for me please? For the journey. It's only about twenty minutes, but if I can get them to chill and eat on the way there, I'll feel loads better.'

He dutifully runs to both stables and grabs the haynets out of each, before standing back and watching me as I begin walking Hattie into her side. She's a little hesitant, but as I suspected, she follows Lincoln with relative ease. Eddie puts the back bar up across her, and while she flinches a little, she's pretty good. I'm so impressed with her and how she's responding – she's doing so well.

I tie them both up, and Eddie jumps on via the groom's door and starts tying the haynets too. I squeeze out from underneath him, putting my hands on his waist as I do, and in spite of the incredible stress and upset that's coursing through me right now, I still can't help but feel that electricity, that connection with him. I notice him look down at me out of the corner of his eye. I know he feels it too; he doesn't need to say. It's as present as the air we breathe.

I love him but I just can't tell him yet.

I run around to the back of the trailer and lift the ramp. It's as light as a feather. Sarah keeps her trailer in such good condition that's it no surprise really.

Eddie runs into the barn and closes both stable doors before switching off the lights. I'm locking the groom's door as he comes back. He stops to kiss me on the cheek, checking the locks are across both the trailer ramp and the groom's door, before he makes sure I'm in with my seat belt on.

And just like that, we're off. I'm taking Lincoln and Hattie away, as quickly as I can before any more harm can come to them.

Alice's field is checked multiple times a day. It's on her parents' property, so I know that not only will they be safe, but they'll never be found by Angel or her brothers. The feeling of relief as we leave the yard is huge.

Hattie travels fairly well. There are a few neighs from Lincoln and a few stamps as we come to a halt at traffic lights, but that's about it. The journey is pretty smooth, and by the time we get to the field, it's completely pitch black. I use my phone light – it's all I have with me – and find the key safe by the main gate lock. Thankfully, I know it well from helping Alice out over the years.

Before swinging the gate open, Eddie unlocks the front ramp and lowers it. Lincoln comes off first, with his head in the air. He's probably wondering where the bloody hell he is. Hattie swiftly follows in Eddie's hands, as she gets agitated being on the trailer alone. I hear horses in the distance and quickly open the gate enough for us to walk them both in. We whip the headcollars off both and step back, closing the gate as we hear hooves thundering across the field in the dark.

Jack and Alfie are two huge draft horses. Alfie is a full Clydesdale. He's huge, and at just five years old and a hair over eighteen hands, I always tease Alice that he's going to make well over nineteen. He won't. I highly doubt it anyway, but I love seeing the look on her face when she starts mentally pricing up bigger rugs, specially made tack and an even bigger lorry.

Jack isn't anywhere near as big, but that's because he's half Clydesdale, half warmblood. He's seventeen hands, and while a big horse, much like Lincoln, he looks minuscule in comparison to Alfie.

Both Jack and Alfie are here now, sniffing Lincoln and Hattie. Everyone's grown about a hand taller as they all inspect each other. Hattie seems surprisingly calm being in a brand-new field with two completely new horses. She snorts but that's it.

It's like it signals that everything's OK, because as soon as she does, they all turn and run off into the darkness. They're safe here; I don't need to worry about them. They're going to be fine.

Eddie puts his arm around me, having locked the gate back up. He takes the key out of my hands and puts it back into the safe. 'They're fine now, Jen. You don't need to worry now.'

I throw my arms around his waist and enjoy the darkness. The peace is beautiful. Is it crazy to say I feel safe here? Here in the darkness. Or is it a case of feeling safe in his arms?

Looking out into the distance, I think of what it was like in that stable. Dark, cold and alone. I look into the field that's now a temporary home for Lincoln and Hattie, and remember all I saw from that stable door was an old office with a dingy light and that water-tower thing.

I wonder what it was, a water tower or an old, disused windmill? Either way, it just sat there, surrounded by nothing. It took up so much of the view, yet no one but me seems to have paid it any mind.

And that's when it hits me... that thing. Could that be what we've been looking for this whole time? Would that house something below ground – the place their whole operation is running from?

My body must stiffen because Eddie looks at me. 'What's the matter?'

'I need to call Tristan. I think I know where to look for them.'

ELEVEN

I SPEND the next twenty minutes in the car explaining to Tristan that I think I might have a clue. His confusion is no surprise considering I don't even know what I'm talking about. 'It's a windmill, like a broken one, or some sort of water tower or, you know, one of those silo things that the farmers put stuff in. You know?'

'Gorgeous, I don't have a fucking clue what you're on about.'

'Just get that copper on the phone and tell him to meet us where we were earlier.'

'How will we even see it from there in the dark?'

'Because it was lit up. When I was there, it was lit up and was all I could see. Why would it have been lit up unless people needed to see it, needed to be able to know where it was?'

'OK, I'll call him now and make my way there. Who are you with?'

'I'm with Eddie.'

'OK, just stay safe, alright?'

'I will.'

We pull up at the yard, and Eddie swings his truck round before expertly reversing the trailer back into the front of the barn. He whips the lock back on and I run the key back into the feed room. I give Zara and Scrappy one last check over to make sure everything's OK and come out to find Eddie finishing up a phone call.

I'm suddenly worried that I've just given the enemy our next move and can't help but worry that I've read him wrong this whole time.

'Maybe we should go in separate cars?'

'What the fuck are you on about? Why? Jen, I'm not leaving you. We're going together. Get in the fucking truck now.'

I wonder whether I'm making the right decision, but as always, I go with my gut when it comes to Eddie, and it's telling me to go with him.

After a somewhat awkward journey in which I spend the entire time talking to myself, asking myself questions and providing myself with not a single answer, we arrive at the desolate yard. Instead of being wary and worried, however, this time I barely let the truck come to a stop before jumping out. I race to the stable where I found myself that night and stare toward it.

Tristan is already there, with two police officers. Eddie follows behind me and I see another car pull up.

A WPC gets out along with a police dog.

'Bloody hell, Tristan, this was just a hunch. Why have you called the entire cavalry?'

'I didn't call her, gorgeous. I think your boy might have done.' He nods toward Eddie, who's now in deep conversation with her, pointing toward the broken windmill thing in front of us. It must be 500 yards ahead, maybe more. We won't be able to walk there in the dark, across the fields. We'll never see in front of us. Thankfully, Clements seems to think we'll be able to drive there. If it is the place, they'd need to be able to get vehicles in and out, which means we should be able to as well.

I jump in the car with Clements, with Tristan in the front passenger seat.

Eddie is close behind in his truck, as is the WPC, who's now on her phone. Has he been working with the police all along?

Arriving at the base of this thing, Tristan tells me, after a little googling on his phone, that he's concluded it's an old disused silo. We pull up and find it lit up from outside and that an entrance has been made in the side. It's clearly a makeshift job, and not a great one at that.

Before Tristan and I get near the door handle, not even considering what might be on the other side, Clements and Eddie push us back. 'Get back in the car.'

There are more officers on their way we're told, and, within seconds, two vans and three cars pull up. All unmarked, all silent.

Tristan and I are put into the back of one of the vans as they burst in, and we're left to watch from behind bullet-proof glass as officer after officer runs in with taser guns and more. Two police dogs follow in pursuit, and then there's silence.

No shouting. We hear nothing. We simply sit in silence. Tristan holds my hand and sits back in his chair, crossing his legs and looking up to the ceiling of the van. He isn't watching. I wonder if he's thinking of his mum – the one person he's been doing this for this entire time.

Then, slowly but surely, police officers appear from the side door, two by two, each pair accompanying a dissolved-looking person. I don't recognise most of them, until they bring Angel out. I see her face. I thought she'd be angry, but she looks anything but. She looks relieved.

Angel is swiftly followed by Damion, Liv's ex, who's being manhandled as he throws himself about on the ground, trying his hardest to get away from them. I wonder if Alfie Drafter will follow suit, and sure enough, there he is. The older of the two brothers, Alfie comes easily. He doesn't throw himself around. He doesn't cause a fuss. He knows he's been caught and it's a simple as that.

Everyone removed is placed in cuffs and put into the back of the other van, as yet more police officers turn up.

I feel somewhat in shock about it all. It's over. It's finally over.

'Well would you look at that. Jen Seaton, journalist extraordinaire, cracks it. How do you feel?'

'I don't know in all honesty. I'm not entirely sure how I should feel. Apart from in shock. They came out so quietly. That's it? I was expecting more drama with it all.'

Tristan giggles to himself. 'Were you wanting a car chase or a hostage situation perhaps?'

'Well maybe not but something. Is that really it?'

'I'd say aside from the trial, yes. That's really it. You found it, Jen. I'm just disappointed it took you being drugged and kidnapped for it to happen.'

I look out the windows and watch Eddie. He's shaking hands with police officers. Someone says thank you, from what I can gather, and he's being patted on the back.

He was working with them. All those times he pleaded with me to just give him more time. They were on to them already. He just needed exactly the same as us, the location, and then they would have them. And that's exactly what I gave him.

Everything Angel ever said was a lie. He was always telling the truth. Always.

TWELVE

I LOOK AT EDDIE, still in shock. He's talking to two policemen like he knows them, like he's one of them. I'm still trying to gather exactly what's happened, but all I know is that this is quite possibly behind us.

I watch him, looking more authoritative than I've ever seen before. He almost looks a little relieved. He's in deep discussion, moving his gaze from different areas around this silo thing to the desolate yard we left behind. He's pointing at Tristan, pointing toward the stables, at Angel, who's currently sat wrapped in a foil blanket, and then to me. When his eyes meet mine, he stops talking for a moment. He's gathering his thoughts. He finally tears his gaze away and points to the notepad that one of the policeman is making notes in before giving him a pat on the shoulder. They smile at each other before shaking hands, and he turns toward me.

He takes a few steps toward me before stopping and taking a deep breath. He cocks his head to the side and the usual cheeky grin I see when he gets out of his truck before our usual appointments begins to show, slowly creeping across his face. I can't help but mirror his smile. It must give him the signal that it's OK to pass go, because he sees me and resumes his slow and steady walk toward me as I peel myself off the side of the van that I've leant on for support for the last thirty minutes.

He must be trying to gather his thoughts or figure out what he's going to say. Like he's ever needed to think about it before – he usually just says whatever's on the tip of his tongue.

'So...'

'So...'

'When you said to trust you, in a few weeks, it'll all be over... what you meant was: give us a hand, Jen; I can't do it without you.'

'Oh for fuck's sake.' His smile grows even more as he wraps an arm around my shoulder. 'Thank you, Jen, I couldn't have done it without you.' The sarcastic tone is there in every word he utters.

'How long have you been working with them – the police I mean?'

'A little while.'

'Is that all I'm getting? After all of this shit, you're still playing Mr Vague?'

His grip around me tightens as he orders, 'Follow me.' We walk toward a bench that's barely sitting upright and both plant ourselves down with caution, making sure it holds up underneath our weight before fully committing to our seat.

'So, many moons ago, I applied to be a police officer. I'd been a farrier for a while and had, you know, worked with the Drafters. But I wanted out. I wanted a fresh start. I wanted a better life, and being a copper seemed like the logical step toward getting myself on a good path I guess. It felt on the straight and narrow. The only trouble was, I'd got myself into a spot of bother previously with the arseholes that are Angel's brothers. It was an immediate no because of my record. Then about a year ago, the Met got back in touch. They propositioned me. Offered me a way to get out and wipe the slate clean, so to speak.'

'Propositioned you how?'

'I'm guessing my name came up in previous investigations with these guys and they recognised it from my application. I don't know for sure. All I know is that when I was approached, I was as petrified as I was relieved. Those guys are capable of some pretty shady shit. I worried they'd find out what I was doing, but at the same time, it wasn't me. It only began so I could help my mum, and it spiralled out of control. I was suddenly so heavily involved in this hell, and I couldn't see a way out.

'This was offering me that way out. I had to barter to get Angel out with me, but they eventually agreed once I told them how it all started.'

I slouch back in my chair and look to the sky. 'Why were you so insistent on wanting to help her? Especially after what she did to me.'

'Jen, after what she did to you at Hogan's, my help for her stopped. Before that though, I couldn't ignore what they were doing to her. She had no one. Not a soul. Only me. That's why I allowed all the shit she used to pull. They would let her out every so often when they needed her on side again or when they had a particularly important buyer coming to town. That's why you'd see her in Hogan's or out competing. That was her only escape and always cheered her up, which made it much easier for them to get her to do what they wanted. Other than that, she was pimped out here, there and everywhere. She was essentially being raped multiple times a week. I can't speak for her, but from what I saw of her over the years, it did things to her. To her mind.

'I know she's sorry for what she did…'

I immediately interject before he tries to explain a way out for her, putting my hands up to stop him speaking. 'I don't care. I don't want to know. She assisted in abducting me. She spiked my drink and abducted me, leaving me on a stone floor in a stable in the middle of nowhere. If I hadn't got away, I dread to think what the fuck they would have done to me.'

'I don't want to think about that either. I'm just telling you why the fuck she's so…well, fucked. Obviously after she did that, the bargaining to get her out with me sort of went out the window. She'll be charged.'

He turns his head toward Angel. I follow his gaze and see that her hands are being removed from the foil blanket that's currently wrapped around her and her wrists are being adorned with cuffs. It makes me both happy and a little sad at the same time.

'I'm guessing your mates over there will give her a much leaner sentence thanks to you though?'

'Quite possibly. I'll never forgive her for what she did you to. Ever.' He squeezes my hand and places it on his knee, looking down at our now linked fingers. 'But she's been abused for years. They drove her to the things that she did.'

I sit back and look to the sky once more, wondering where on earth we go from here.

A few policemen help Angel to her feet and escort her to one of the cars. They open the door and, just like they do in the films, one of them pops a hand on top of her head as she sits herself in the back seat. She doesn't look angry; she doesn't look sorry. She almost looks at peace, as if she's just glad to be out of her brothers' clutches. I can't say I blame her. Before the car pulls away, she smiles sweetly at Eddie and begins to cry.

He just looks at her and eventually gives her a nod as the car starts to move.

There's a tie between the two of them, I can't deny that, but true to his word, they weren't in a relationship. They were, and indeed still very much are, complicated. He was her one escape, her one protector in a world of violence and sexual assault. No wonder she was as possessive over him as she was. I'll never forgive her for what she did, but I will move on. I understand at least.

'How you doing, gorgeous?'

I look up to see Tristan's usual beaming smile looking down at me. Eddie's hand instantly begins to stiffen, but I give him a squeeze, telling him to cool it.

'I'm not bad. Better now. So... did you know about Eddie?'

'I had a feeling. You think I'd have been involved in this case for as long as I have without finding out a few little titbits along the way? I had a feeling he was helping the police, but I just couldn't find out any more than that. You, on the other hand, totally different story. You had no idea yet went with your gut anyway. I'm impressed. And you knocked it out the park. Granted, I'd much rather you hadn't been kidnapped in order to find this place but you know... every cloud and all that.'

Eddie rises, with anger across his face. 'You put her in danger.'

'I gave her a job. She knew the dangers involved. Yet you continued keeping her in the dark this whole time. I think you'll find, Edward, you put her in danger.'

I stand and put myself between them. This is ridiculous.

'You both realise I'm not a fucking child, don't you? Tristan, you gave me the story of a lifetime. I'll be writing up an incredible exposé with my name at the fucking top. I couldn't be happier. Eddie! Yes, you kept me in the dark, but I get it, you had to. This wasn't an ideal situation for anyone, but here we are. So let's crack on, shall we? Besides, I'm bloody starving.'

We spent the rest of our time there talking with police officers before Tristan and I leave. We're taken back by Clements who's now far less prickly. Eddie wasn't too happy about it, but we had to get back to the office. I needed to get down as much information as I possibly could about this whole... thing, adventure whatever you could call it. Tristan also wanted to discuss the legalities of the story. What I could write, what I couldn't right now, before a trial would take place. He then spent a great deal of time telling me how these things usually played out in court, something else I'd not only get to see but would have to take part in, giving evidence. My career had changed almost overnight. This was all I'd ever wanted, but for some reason, I still didn't feel completely happy and I knew exactly why.

'Tristan, I need to get home. I'm pretty much done for the day. I'm knackered and...'

'And you have someone to see, gorgeous.'

I look at him, a little perplexed. Is this flirting just a game to him or is he genuinely disappointed?

'Don't worry, gorgeous, I can see the cogs turning. I'm OK. My heart's a little bruised that you want to dash off and see that brute of a man.'

He feigns a sad face and clutches his chest, pretending

to grip his, I'm gathering, broken one before his face breaks out in a huge smile.

'Honestly, my love, take the rest of the evening off and go see your knight in shining armour. You deserve it.'

'You were pretty good yourself, you know?'

'Oh I know, and I'm going to tell your friend Liv all about it at Hogan's tonight. I'm going to tell her all about my tough day fighting the bad guys. See if she feels sorry enough for me to shag the shit out of me.'

'You cheeky sod! When did you two start chatting?'

'I might have got talking to her at the hospital when I tried to come in and see you.'

Just as I'd thought!

He winks at me and ends the conversation with, 'See you in the morning. We'll talk then.'

Ominous, but I don't hang around to find out what it is we'll be talking about. I need to get out of here.

I grab my bag and start making my way down the stairs. There's a cab office not too far from the paper so I decide to chuck a left as I make my way out of the reception door – and find myself walking face first into a rock-hard chest.

'Shit. I'm—' It's Eddie. I expel a loud burst of air as I realise it's him. Of course it's him. Who else would it be?

'I wanted to come and see you, make sure you were OK. See if you needed a lift home?'

'Are you done playing cops and robbers?' I smile at him. I'm ecstatic if I'm honest.

'Until tonight.'

'What do you mean?'

'Put it this way, I have a feeling that sharp tongue of yours is going to get you in trouble when we get back to the flat.'

'Is that a threat, Eddie?'

'Might be.' His grip on me tightens, and I can't help but let out a squeal as he grabs my waist and hurries me back to his truck. I have a feeling tonight, I'm going to be pretty busy.

As we sit in the truck on the way back to mine, the sexual tension is palpable, but I still find time to text Liv.

Jen: You cheeky minx! Tristan eh!?

Liv: Cannot fucking wait to shag the crap out of that man!

I laugh out loud.

'What's so funny?'

'Nothing. Well not nothing. But I think Tristan's about to meet his match...'

THIRTEEN

AFTER A NIGHT with very little sleep, mainly down to Eddie keeping me up all night, I kiss him goodbye and watch him walk down my stairwell and out of the building. I have a twinge of something. I don't know. Maybe I miss him already? Either way, I want to get back to work to find out what's going on. Where we go from here. Is this it? After this story, is my time at the paper done?

I grab a cup of tea on my way in, nipping through the drive-through in my beat-up car and walk straight into the office like I've been here for years. I don't want to leave this place.

I head straight to Tristan's office to find him sitting at his desk.

'Hey.' I give a little wave as I chuck my bag to the floor and slump into the chair on the opposite side of the desk.

He hands me an envelope without saying a word. Opening it up, I wonder if it's a cheque for the work I've done, but instead I pull out a contract. He's offering me a full-time position at the paper.

I'm stunned. In silence. Not sure of what to say.

Considering I'm supposed to be the queen of words, it's unexpected. For him too I'm guessing.

'So how do you feel, gorgeous? Pretty excited to be doing what you've always wanted?'

'How do you know I'm going to sign the contract?' I cock an eyebrow. When it comes to Tristan, I like to keep him on his toes, but truth be told, I couldn't be happier. I just don't want to make it too obvious to him. He's become a great friend after everything we've been through, though, after everything I've done for this story, for this huge headline, I deserve this position.

Fuck modesty. I was bloody amazing, carrying on as I did after what happened.

I would have been shocked if he hadn't offered me a job.

'Yeah, it's pretty good, I won't lie. But after the work I delivered, I deserve no less... perhaps a little more even?'

'Oh God, what? What do you want? A shag?'

'Piss off, you know I'm not interested. Besides, I heard you're all shagged out after last night.'

'Ha! I forgot women talk, don't they? I can't believe she'd use me like that and then gossip about it with you.' He pouts in an attempt to look vaguely upset, but unfortunately for him, he struggles to keep the grin off his face for long. What he doesn't know is that I've been updated constantly by Liv, telling me what a gentleman he was and the wonderful things he's been texting her this morning. They're a match made in heaven, but he and I will always have this flirtation. It's harmless. Fun but harmless, and something that Liv would very much approve of. There's no doubt about that. Eddie, on the other hand, may be a different story entirely.

'You and I work very well together, love, and I intend on keeping that up. I'm glad to have you here at the paper.

Granted, I'd have loved to have paid you a lot less, but I guess I've got to give you something for being kidnapped or whatever the fuck it is you're going to moan about now.'

He rolls his eyes, then stares at me, cocking his eyebrow, inviting me to say something more. 'So what is it? What do you want?'

'An office. I want my own office.'

'Oh, gorgeous! Come with me...'

He stands up and rounds his desk, takes my hand and leads me out through his glass doors. We walk virtually two metres to the left, where I'm met with yet more shining glass and, more importantly, a man attaching a name to the glass... Jen Seaton, Senior Journalist.

'You're second in command to me and only me. You didn't think I'd put you through the wringer and then not reward you? I can't have my senior journalist not having her own office, can I? Wouldn't look very professional.'

'I'm... I'm speechless.'

'Well you'll have to do better than that, love, you're a fucking writer.'

His grin is huge but it disappears in an instant, and he stands in front of me, square and tall. His face becomes serious, and he reaches out his hand to shake mine.

'Welcome to my team, Jen. I'm incredibly chuffed to have someone of your abilities working at this paper. I cannot wait to see what you're going to do here. I have extremely high hopes for you, and I genuinely believe this is just the start of a very exciting career.'

I shake his hand with vigour, trying my best to ward off the tears, but with glassy eyes only manage a very weak, 'Thank you.'

I look at the office and then look back to him. He nods toward the door, and I walk in and sit myself down. It's a small office, but much like my small flat, it's all mine and I couldn't be happier.

'There's some space on the walls for your artwork, oh and I thought this could be the first piece to go up...' He whips a cloth off of something hanging on the wall to reveal a mock-up of my very first front page. The story of the Drafter brothers and how I – and Tristan of course – found the location of their operation, ultimately putting an end to one of the biggest drug rings in Essex.

'Thank you. Thank you for everything.'

'Anytime, gorgeous! I had someone in IT whip it up quickly. Of course, the real cover will be up there shortly, but I thought this would look good for you coming in and seeing your new office. Remember, this is only the beginning.'

I look down at the desk and run my hand along the leather that sits on top of it. My arms are stretched out to either far corner when I look up at him with quite possibly the cheekiest grin he's ever seen.

'Oh shit, what?'

'Can I have a day off?'

He rolls his eyes and walks off, shouting over his shoulder, 'Fuck off and I'll see you Monday, bright and breezy, love, but I want something sent into me by tomorrow morning at the latest. Shag him as much as you want, but get me something! I'm not paying you the big bucks for nothing, gorgeous.'

I take one last look at my front page, hung proudly on the wall, and grab my bag. Before I can step foot outside the office however, I run face first into a huge bouquet. I really should start looking where I'm going.

The bouquet is filled with off-white avalanche roses, my favourite. Behind them is the man I've always loved.

'What are you doing here?' My voice is stupidly high from the excitement of seeing him, and he knows it too.

'I wanted to congratulate you, and Tristan sent me a text saying you'd be getting off early, so I figured I'd come pick you up and take you out to celebrate your new job.'

His smile is as wicked as it is mischievous. Tristan must have told him what he was doing before he told me. That's why he didn't mind saying goodbye this morning, because he knew he'd be seeing me in just a couple of hours. I couldn't be happier that he's doing this, but right now, my thoughts are elsewhere.

'Now while I'd love to go out for some food...'

'Let me guess, you've got somewhere else to be? Do I get a prize for guessing where that is?'

'No.' And just like that, I take his one free hand and start walking him out of the office, down the stairwell and out of the front doors. We head to my car, and I look at him with pleading eyes as I turn the ignition. He knows exactly where we're going and I'm giving him no time to object. I've got two very important faces to see.

FOURTEEN

I WALK to the gate and call them both. I hear Lincoln nicker from across the field as Eddie shuts the car door behind me. 'Hey, boy, have you missed me?'

He runs straight toward me and leans his head over the gate and into me; he's always happy to see me. Today, however, I'm not going to make him work. Today, I'm going to leave him to play in the field with his friends. Today, someone else needs a little more attention.

'I'm taking you home tomorrow, dude, so enjoy your last day of freedom.'

I hear the others walking up behind him. The only sounds are his breathing and the sound of their shoes on the hardcore that leads to the field entrance. He nuzzles me once more before turning around and facing the others. He waits for me to step backward, away from the gate, before he bucks, farts and bolts into the middle of the field.

He's a good boy, and he's my good boy.

The only one left standing by the gate is Hattie. I feel deflated at the sight of her. I don't know why my feelings have suddenly changed.

Eddie looks toward me, confusion all over his face. 'Why so glum?'

'I can afford her now, no problem. But I don't know if I have the time for her? She's going to need a lot of work to get her trust back up.'

She leans over the gate and sniffs me gently, sniffing my face like she did the first night I met her.

'Just to be a normal horse, it's going to take so much time, without even thinking of riding her. I just don't know what to do.'

'I'm sure we can work something out.'

'We?'

'Yes, we. We're a we now. Did I forget to tell you? Besides, she seems to like me – well tolerate me at least. I reckon we can work with her together. She'll come round. After all you've done, after all she's been through, you both deserve to stay together, Jen...' He turns to face me fully, pulls me into him and kisses me – gently, as if he knows he doesn't have to grab what he can, before it's too late. He's kissing me like we aren't being chased, and for once, I appreciate the calmness of it.

He pulls away, looking into my eyes and simply says, 'We deserve to stay together, Jen. You, me, Hattie... and big Lincoln lad over there. What do you think?'

I kiss him back, only this time I kiss him hard, throwing my arms around his neck, practically hanging off of him. And that's all I need to do. The faint scent of farrier smoke that seems to linger around Eddie 24/7 fills my nostrils. I love it, and I love him more.

THE END.

ACKNOWLEDGEMENTS

Well, here we are, back again! I can't believe we've come to the end of the road for Jen & Eddie but I really hope you enjoyed the Soaked Hay Smoke & Mirrors series. I've loved writing it and more than that, I've loved hearing you guys enjoy it so much! Your reviews have been wonderful! But right now, it's time to say thank you to those whom without, I'd never have made it this far.

Of course, it wouldn't be right if I didn't thank the super talented Francessca Wingfield for her incredible talents designing the cover as if she pulled it straight from my mind. Her ability to translate what I'm thinking into an actual cover is beyond amazing!

I'd also like to thank the fabulous Laura Kincaid again. She's been a fantastic copy editor and not to mention, all round fabulous person who puts up with my insecurities and more, when it comes to my manuscripts!

Thank you to my first-class husband! Not only have you been incredibly supportive yet again, while I immerse myself in this story but you've proofread thousands of words, late into the night I might add, and been an wonderful husband and father, allowing me to work and produce this awesome story.

I'd also like to say a huge thank you to my parents for not reading, or at least telling me, they didn't read my previous book. With the steamy scenes and high use of profane language, I'd just like to ask that we continue to pretend you have no idea what's between the covers of my books. Let's remain on this journey to avoid those #awkward moments in life. I love you both very much and I only hope that despite the sometimes 'erotic' nature of the odd scene here and there, you're proud of what I've accomplished.

Writing this acknowledgements page has been a real experience. It's led me to sit back and look at just how far I've come and that wouldn't be possible without you, the reader.

You've left me wonderful reviews on my first book. It's made all the difference and really spurred me on when I've found myself stuck in a rut or dealing with the dreaded writer's block.

You've been wonderful and I only hope the second instalment of this series lived up to your expectations and more. I know it certainly did for me.

I already have some fantastic new series' lined up! I want you to get to know Alice a little more. I dropped a hint about her. Did you pick that up? I'll also be diving deeper into the world of Hattie.

If you follow me on social media, you'll know that Hattie is based on a very real chestnut mare Hattie, my beautiful three year old named Kinsky High Definition. She's my dream horse and a huge work in progress. She's the quirkiest mare I've ever come across but then again, all the good ones are right?

Before I go... If you enjoyed this book, please do leave a

review. It makes a world of difference to little indie authors like myself!

I hope you'll follow my journey as I release my next series but until then, enjoy the wonderful world of horses guys! They're life's natural therapy!

Cover Design: Francessca Wingfield - https://www.facebook.com/FrancesscasPRandDesigns
Editing: Laura Kincaid - https://www.tenthousand.co.uk/
Tea Maker: Rob Hyde - www.fitfob.com

What's Coming Next?

Of course, as you will have realised, this is the end of the story for Jen, Eddie and the Soaked Hay bunch. It was a dream come true to write this series and I hope you've enjoyed it as much as I have! Fear not however as the next two series' I'll be publishing are somewhat intertwined! If you'd like to read more from me, or simply want to find out more about my fabulous equine army, please do sign up to my newsletter or check out my social media links below where I'll be releasing news about forthcoming releases.

I can't wait for you to hear about Alice in a little more detail. I hope you got the hint I dropped there! And I can't wait for you to find out more about Hattie.

Get to know me more here...
Instagram - https://www.instagram.com/thefairweatherrider/
Facebook - https://www.facebook.com/thefairweatherrider
Website - http://thefairweatherrider.com

COPYRIGHT